Deadly Pursuit!

The roan stretched out long legs, Stone sped down the trail, following Kincaid. He rammed his rifle into its scabbard and pulled a Colt.

Kincaid turned for another shot, squeezed the trigger. The gun fired, he couldn't hit Stone, but lead might scare him away. Stone leaned against the roan's mane.

Stone drew closer. Wind whistled through the creases of his old Confederate cavalry hat and washed his cleanly shaven cheeks as he drew a careful bead on Kincaid's back. . . .

*Also in the SEARCHER series by
Josh Edwards*

SEARCHER
LYNCH LAW
TIN BADGE
WARPATH
HELLFIRE
DEVIL'S BRAND
STAMPEDE
RECKLESS GUNS
FORT HAYS BUSTOUT

SEARCHER

BOOM TOWN

Josh Edwards

DIAMOND BOOKS, NEW YORK

This book is a Diamond original edition, and has never been previously published.

BOOM TOWN

A Diamond Book / published by arrangement with the author

PRINTING HISTORY
Diamond edition / November 1992

ISBN: 1-55773-818-1

Diamond Books are published by The Berkley Publishing Group,
200 Madison Avenue, New York, New York 10016.
The name "DIAMOND" and its logo are trademarks
belonging to Charter Communications, Inc.

PRINTED IN THE UNITED STATES OF AMERICA

10 9 8 7 6 5 4 3 2 1

BOOM TOWN

1

THE RUMBLING, CLANGING train roared through a valley carpeted with trees. Far in the distance, the great snow-capped Rocky Mountains lay like jagged teeth against the blue sky. A flock of birds flew past the sun.

John Stone gazed through the window of the railway car. He felt puny, his cares inconsequential. *These mountains will be here long after I'm dust in the wind.*

He sat on the rear seat of the car, back against the wall, facing men and women dressed in eastern finery, others in the rough garb of the frontier. On the opposite side of the aisle, a brunette's eyes struck sparks.

A potbellied stove provided heat. Stone wore a fringed buckskin jacket, his old Confederate cavalry hat hanging on the peg above his head. He was six feet four, two hundred forty pounds. The brunette read a book, traveling alone, not more than eighteen.

Women. He opened his shirt pocket, removed a small daguerreotype picture in a silver frame. A teenaged beauty with light hair gazed at him. His imagination filled in blond tresses, blue eyes, rosy cheeks.

They grew up together on neighboring plantations in South Carolina. The last time he saw her was late 1864, shortly before Sherman's armies devastated the area. When he returned home after the war, she was gone. They said she went west with a Union officer. He'd been searching for her ever since.

1

No woman ever affected him like she. People said he was crazy. He'd tracked her across the Great Plains, brush country of Texas, Arizona desert where Apaches nearly got his hair.

He'd searched, struggled, wandered from town to town, never enough money, most nights spent under the stars. People sent him on wild goose chases, for their perverse amusement. Others provided well-intentioned wrong information. The life drove him to drink. Nearly killed in a hundred saloon brawls. But at last he had a solid lead.

At Fort Hays, Kansas, picked up her trail. They said she left for San Francisco two weeks before with Derek Canfield the gambler. Now Stone was on his way to California, to hunt her down.

She thought he'd been killed in the war. He'd never stopped loving and needing her. At night his bones cried out for her. *Watch out for me, sweetheart. I'm a-comin' on through.*

The train chugged up an incline. The door opened, an outrageous figure in a rumpled filthy white suit appeared: Ray Slipchuck, old stagecoach driver of plains, drunk out of his mind as usual. His pink tongue hung out the side of his mouth, he staggered up the aisle. Passengers cringed, afraid he'd fall on them.

He made his way around the stove, singed his pant leg, remnants of meals on his shirt and tie, a gold chain hung across his stomach. Short, wiry, with a full gray beard, he looked like an aging gopher, but packed a Colt in a low-slung holster. His rusty spur caught the leg of the stove, he tumbled to the floor. Stone grabbed his arm, lifting him as though he were nothing.

"Maybe you should taper off the whiskey, pard. You're out on your feet."

"Time I had me some sleep," Slipchuck said, adjusting the big white cowboy hat on his head.

Stone led him to the bench. Slipchuck fell asleep immediately. They met on a stagecoach in Arizona a few months ago, the wildest old man Stone ever saw. The train slowed as it climbed the steep grade.

Stone's eyes met the brunette's. It weren't for Marie, he'd strike up a conversation. But he'd see Marie soon in San Francisco, didn't need more complications.

Stone looked out the window at a narrow mountain pass rimmed with pine and fir. Modern trains traveled twenty to forty miles an hour in comfort, faster and safer than horseback, but he missed clean air, the big sky.

The transcontinental railroad was a year and a half old. Immigrants poured into the west, built farms and towns. Cattle rode east, to the stockyards of St. Louis, Chicago and New York. The energy and resources of a nation at war now were diverted to the frontier; excitement, adventure, and wealth everywhere, or at least that's what many believed.

The train slowed more, as if coming to a stop. Something wrong? Stone couldn't see anything unusual out the window. Passengers fidgeted. Mechanical difficulty, most probably.

The train came to a sudden halt. Passengers were thrown forward amid shouts and confusion. The far door of the car opened, two men appeared, bandannas covering their faces, guns in hands. "Raise 'em high!"

Stone wore two Colts in crisscrossed gunbelts, slung low and tied down, but they had the drop on him. The outlaws advanced into the car, knuckles white around the butts of their firearms. One, wearing a black bandanna, carried a gunny sack. "Drop yer belongin's in here, nobody'll git hurt."

Red bandanna held his gun on the frightened passengers as black bandanna approached the first eastern dude.

"Empty yer pockets, feller. Ain't got time to play."

The man was pale, lips quivering with terror as he thrust his hands into his pockets. Four masked riders galloped past the car, a shot rang out at the front of the train. A third robber, also wearing a red bandanna, entered the car, gun in hand. He reached to the overhead rack, pulled down a suitcase, rummaged through its contents, found a teak box filled with jewels, tossed it into the bag.

Black bandanna moved toward an elderly farmer, who held a few coins in his hand. "All I got," he said, a note of hope in his voice.

"Toss it in the bag."

An explosion rent the air, the safe in the mail car had been blasted with explosives. Black bandanna held the bag in front of the brunette. She pointed to the topaz heart brooch on her blouse. "It belonged to my mother."

Black bandanna tore it away, she screamed, underclothes exposed. Black bandanna threw her purse into the gunny sack.

The next passenger, a hulking man in work clothes, frowned angrily as the outlaws approached.

"Ain't got all day," black bandanna said.

"Come git it," the passenger replied belligerently.

Black bandanna pulled his trigger. The bark of his gunshot reverberated off the walls of the car. The passenger was hurled back, bitter smoke filled the car. He fell to his back, blood gushing from a hole in his chest.

Red bandanna went through the dead man's pockets as black bandanna held his gunny sack to hands eagerly dropping valuables inside. Green bandanna pulled open the lid of a suitcase. Inside was frilly lady's underwear. "Who belongs to these?"

"I do," said the brunette.

The robber looked her up and down, reached out his black-gloved hand, squeezed her shoulder. Her face went pale. The railway car was silent except for booty dropping into the gunny sack.

"Take your hand off me," the brunette said.

"Make me."

John Stone stepped into the aisle, wearing his old Confederate cavalry hat. Red bandanna drew his gun on him. "Where you think you're goin', asshole?"

"Get away from her."

Green bandanna lifted his hand from the girl's shoulder and moved toward Stone. "How'd you like to die today, cowpoke?"

Stone didn't flinch. The door was thrown open, a stocky man in a black leather vest entered the car, gun in hand. "What's goin' on?"

"Feller there's gittin' frisky."

"Finish yer job. We ain't got all day."

Black vest wore a black bandanna over his face. He turned toward Stone, who noticed a tiny scar like a scimitar at the corner of his left eye. The outlaw chief pulled Stone's guns out of their holsters.

"A man needs his guns," Stone said. "This is injun territory."

"You'll git 'em when we're finished."

Black bandanna tapped Stone's pockets, heard the coins. "Out with 'em."

Stone reached into his pocket and removed nearly a hundred dollars, all his wealth in the world. He let the coins fall into the bag. The robber held it in front of Slipchuck.

"Goddammit," Slipchuck said bitterly, "first time in me life I ever had dinero, the bastards're takin' it away."

Black bandanna laughed, tossed a twenty-dollar gold eagle back at Slipchuck. "Keep this, Pops."

Everybody's gun collected, the last passenger dropped his tinkling coins into the gunny sack. "Let's get out of here," black bandanna said.

The robbers filed out of the car. Passengers dropped to the floor to collect their belongings. The dead man stared lifelessly at the ceiling. The brunette buttoned a blouse over her exposed underclothes.

Stone turned toward the window. A group of outlaws rode past, twin chargers pulling a wagon loaded with loot. Their black-vested chief led them toward a mountain trail.

Stone walked out the door, jumped to the ground, saw a stack of guns lying near a car two lengths down. He ran toward it, as other passengers stepped from train platforms. Stone searched through the pile of revolvers and derringers, a small arsenal. At least they left the guns, a decent human gesture considering Shoshonis roamed the area.

He found his Colts and checked the loads as a crowd of passengers gathered around. They searched for their guns; Stone looked down the road where the gang rode. Probably a hideout in the mountains.

"They got the gold shipment!" A short, stout conductor ran toward them. "Killed the guards!"

Stone holstered his guns. "Excuse me," said a female voice. He turned to the brunette. "Thank you for standing up for me. My name's Gail Petigru."

He touched his forefinger to the brim of his hat. "John Stone. Traveling alone?"

"I'm visiting my sister in Lodestone. How about you?"

"I was on my way to San Francisco, but guess I'll have to stop in Lodestone to raise funds."

"Do you know anyone in Lodestone?"

"Not a soul."

"My brother-in-law is a banker. Perhaps he'll be able to help you."

Slipchuck joined them, an expression of disgust on his face. "They even took me bloody watch!"

"My partner, Ray Slipchuck," Stone said, introducing the old historian of the West.

Slipchuck raised his hat. "Whenever I want to find John Stone, I jest look fer the purtiest gal, and thar he is."

Stone cleared his throat. Slipchuck realized he said the wrong thing again. The engineer walked toward them, wearing a scarred leather apron and billed cap. "Better git movin'," he said. "Injuns live 'round here."

Passengers returned to the train. Stone moved Gail Petigru's baggage to the rear of the car with his. She sat opposite him on an upholstered bench. His long sprawling legs almost touched hers. Slipchuck pulled out the twenty-dollar golden eagle. "Don't know about you-all," he said, "but I need a drink."

He moved unsteadily toward the parlor car, leaving Stone with Gail Petigru. She examined him at close range, weather-beaten features with scars and fresh bruises, dark blond hair, not bad-looking.

The train jerked, Gail fell forward. Stone held her shoulders. The train lurched up the hill. Gail returned to her seat. He had tremendous strength in his hands. "Were you in the war?"

"Long time ago." He paused. "Where you coming from?"

"Maine. How about you?"

"South Carolina originally."

"What do you do?"

"A little this, a little that."

"I just graduated from Bradford College. Did you ever go to college?"

"Long time ago."

"What'd you study?"

"Don't remember."

The train gathered speed. Often he ran into pretty women, but generally remained faithful to Marie. What about this time? Gail Petigru was sweet and innocent. Leave her alone.

"Should be in Lodestone by suppertime," she said. "Supposed to be an interesting place."

"Mining town, I understand."

"Growing by leaps and bounds. Even have their own police department. Where will you live?"

"Damned if I know."

"Maybe you can stay with my sister and brother-in-law. They've got lots of room."

"They don't know me, neither do you. For all you know, I'm a worse outlaw than the men who were here."

"I'm a good judge of people. I know you're not an outlaw. You're a southern gentleman. Do you have a profession?"

"Not that I know of."

"What's your purpose in life?"

"Looking for somebody."

The train leveled off. Passengers grumbled about the robbery. "A detachment of soldiers should travel with every train!"

"How long's your sister been living in Lodestone?" Stone asked Gail.

"Two years. It's the fastest growing city in Colorado, after Denver. I can't wait to see it."

Slipchuck sat in the parlor car, glass of whiskey in one hand, cheroot in the other. His eyes half-closed, he stared out the window at a mountain peak wreathed in clouds.

All his life he wanted to go to Frisco. They said it had the best whorehouses in the world. Almost there, his trip cut short by a bunch of outlaws, the common man can't git an even break. *Instead I'm a-goin' to a mining town—high prices, thieves in every shadow, garbage in the streets.*

"Aren't you a friend of the gentleman who stood up to the outlaws?" asked a British accent in a blue suit.

"What's it to you?"

"Is he a professional gunfighter?"

Slipchuck was drunk, his tongue ran away with him. "He ain't no perfeshional, but he's got the fastest hands I ever seen."

"Where can I find him?"

"Look fer the prettiest gal on the train."

Stone dozed in his seat, head rolling gently with the motion of the train. Gail Petigru gazed at him. He was mysterious, moody, a lost puppy dog, and something more she didn't want to think about.

"Sir?"

A man stood over Stone, shaking his shoulder. Stone opened his eyes.

"Are you John Stone? I work for Mr. Tobias Moffitt, an official of this railroad. He'd like to speak with you."

Stone remembered the special luxury car hitched in front of the caboose. A vice president of the Kansas Pacific traveling to San Francisco with family and friends. "What about?"

"A job."

Stone unlimbered from the seat and put on his hat. He tapped Gail on the knee. "Let's see what a private car looks like."

He grabbed her hand and pulled her up. She followed willy-nilly down the aisle, his grip like steel. They passed startled passengers, entered the next car. Passengers stared at them. Slipchuck appeared, on his way back from the bar.

"Where the hell you goin'?" Slipchuck asked, leaning perilously to one side.

Stone placed his arm around Slipchuck's shoulder. "We've got a job."

The strange procession entered the parlor car, robbery victims glanced at them. Slipchuck tried to act dignified, but tripped over a doctor's black bag, flew down the aisle, hit the stovepipe, cracked it apart. A pound of black granular soot fell onto his white suit.

The next door led to the private car. Stevenson, the British butler, hit the knocker. A small window in the door opened, two beady eyes appeared. A moment later the door opened. A man in a railroad conductor's uniform stood at the entrance.

"This way, please."

Red velvet curtains hung over the windows, walls paneled with mahogany. Well-dressed people sat in an opulent living room. Stevenson stopped before a man with a face like a bulldog. Two large eyes turned down at the corners examined Stone. "Come here."

Stone walked toward him. "This is Mr. Moffitt," Stevenson said, "vice president of the Kansas Pacific Railroad."

Mr. Moffitt hooked his thumbs in his suspenders. "Understand you stood up to those outlaws back there. Are you a professional?"

"No, sir."

"Where'd you get that hat?"

"Long time ago."

"Still fighting the war?"

"Not me."

Slipchuck teetered forward, covered with soot. "He ain't no perfeshional, but you're a-lookin' at the man what shot Tod Buckalew!"

Moffitt shrugged. "Who's Tod Buckalew?"

On the opposite side of the table, a gray-haired man spoke. "Tod Buckalew was a fast gun from Kansas, some say the fastest."

Moffitt narrowed one eye as he looked up at Stone. "I need a bodyguard between here and Lodestone. I'll pay ten dollars in cash when the train pulls into the station."

"Don't work alone." Stone placed his arm around Slipchuck's shoulder, and Slipchuck nearly collapsed onto the floor. "Need this man to watch my back. You may be interested to know he's the man who shot Frank Quarternight."

Slipchuck held his palm up modestly. "A lucky shot, caught him on his blind side. But Johnny here shot *Dave* Quarternight, and they say he was a damn sight faster'n his brother Frank."

"I wouldn't be here right now," Stone said, "it weren't for this man. If you hire me, got to hire him."

The ladies and gentlemen at the round table stared at the duo as if they came from Mars. "Extraordinary," an old dowager croaked, through the lenses of her lorgnette.

"I'll pay the old fellow five dollars," Moffitt said.

"He gets what I get," Stone replied, "or no deal."

"Ten dollars for this?"

Slipchuck slapped iron, Moffitt stared down the barrel of a Colt. A woman let out a tiny scream. "Now see here," said one of the men at the table.

Moffitt went pale. The cigar trembled in his hand. Slipchuck winked, dropped his Colt back into his holster.

"Ten dollars a day for each man," Moffitt said. His eyes fell on Gail goggling oil paintings, upholstered furniture, crystal chandeliers. "What can I do for you, young lady?"

"I'm with him."

Every male eye on the railroad car turned to her, while women sensed a dangerous rival. Mr. Moffitt took her hand and moved her to the center of the car. "Who might you be?"

"I'm on my way to Lodestone, where my sister lives, and this man protected me from a robber who tore my clothes."

They returned their eyes to John Stone.

"When do we start?" he asked.

"Right now." Moffitt turned to Stevenson. "Take care of them."

Stevenson led them to the center of the car. "Have you eaten?"

"Not for a while," Stone replied.

They followed him to the dining room. A Negro woman in an apron brought them a tray of chicken sandwiches. They heard the easterners talking in the other part of the car.

"Never heard of Quarternight," said the tall, gray-haired man, "but Tod Buckalew was a terror. Killed eight men, and he was only in his early twenties when he got shot."

"Hope we haven't let the fox into the chicken coop," muttered another man nervously. "We really don't know who he is, and he's armed to the teeth."

Moffitt's voice came to them. "She has a face of an angel."

"What about the old codger?"

Slipchuck reached for his gun. Stone placed his hand on the old man's bony wrist. "Don't even think about it."

"You git a little gray hair, people think you cain't cut it no more. Let me tell you something. There was this little whore back at Hays City, and I . . ."

Stone cleared his throat. "There's a lady present."

"Don't pay any attention to me," Gail said with a wave of her hand. "Speak your mind."

"Wa'al," Slipchuck said, "lemme put it this way. When I was finished, she said I did it better'n some younger men."

Gail blanched. Stone munched his sandwich. The door at the far end of the railway car opened, and a conductor shouted: "One hour to Lodestone!"

2

THE TRAIN PULLED into Lodestone at dusk. Moffitt and his entourage debarked first, into the waiting arms of the mayor, city council, and Ladies Auxiliary. A twenty-piece uniformed band blared a ceremonial march, flags fluttered in the breeze.

Moffitt hooked one thumb in a suspender, held his Corona cigar in his other hand, and said, "Never have I met such a warm welcome in all my born days!" The same line he'd used in every train stop from New York City.

Mayor Ralston wore a flowing white mustache and derby hat slanted low over his eyes. He shook Moffitt's hand, to wild applause. "Sir," he said, "we're proud to have you in our town! May I remind you, Lodestone is the fastest growing community west of the Mississippi! We have the richest soil, hardest workers, most forward-looking and inspiring community leaders, and loveliest women in the world! On behalf of all citizens, I welcome you to Lodestone, King of the Rockies!"

The crowd cheered, Stone stepped off the train. He checked the terrain like a cavalry officer planning an advance. Tall ghostly buildings spread across a valley, surrounded by a wasteland of rotting tree stumps on nearby hills and mountains. A terrible stench filled the air, the stamp mill pounded steadily in the foothills. On the other side of the train station, a man in a blue uniform stood on a ladder and lit a lamp suspended from a varnished pole, street full of wagons and horses to their shins in muck.

11

Stone hadn't seen anything like this since Kansas City. Slipchuck tugged his shirt sleeve. "Where the hell you goin', pard?"

"Aren't we looking for a hotel?"

"How you know what hotel to go to?"

"I thought we'd walk down the street and look around."

"You'll end up in a shithole full of the worse riffraff and backstabbers in the territory. Only way to find the best hotel, ask some upstandin' citizens. Best place to find upstandin' citizens is the best saloon. You stick with me, I'll show you how it's done."

Slipchuck walked ahead forthrightly, saddlebags over his shoulder, spurs clanging, passing ladies, gentlemen, miners in filthy clothes, eyes bleary with fatigue. They came to an alley. A man sat with an empty bottle in his hand. Slipchuck shook the drunkard's shoulder. "Wake up!"

The drunkard opened his eyes.

"What's the best saloon in town?"

"Graaaaannnd. Paaaalllaaacce."

The drunkard collapsed against the wall, exhausted by his effort. Slipchuck strolled to the sidewalk and buttonholed the first man he saw. "Which way to the Grand Palace?"

"Down the street, left at the first corner."

Slipchuck stopped to ogle a little blonde. He had a weakness for little blondes. Stone lifted him by the scruff of his neck and carried him a few paces, then set him down again. They passed a barbershop, pawnshop, and bakery. Halfway down the next street, a huge lighted sign said GRAND PALACE.

The saloon and casino occupied most of the block. Lanterns shone in windows, the sound of a band could be heard. Slipchuck stopped in his tracks. "Now *that's* what I call a saloon!"

"We already passed six hotels."

"You'd wake up in the mornin' with a bullet in your head."

A deputy in blue uniform and badge walked past. On his head was a funny cap with a shiny black visor, similar to the one worn by the railroad conductor. Slipchuck plunged into the traffic, dirty white pants absorbing muck like a blotter. Stone's dark blue britches were tucked into his boots, cavalry style, each boot carried a knife. They reached the sidewalk in front of the veranda running the full length of the building. Four doors were crowded with patrons coming and going, others sat at tables, waited upon by a small troop of men in white shirts and black vests.

Slipchuck ambled toward the closest door. Stone followed him, stepped out from the backlight. An immense area stretched before him, filled with people of every description, bars, dance floor in back, chuck-a-luck wheels spinning around, flight of stairs leading to the second floor. He'd seen smaller barns.

"What's yer pleasure, gents?" asked the bartender, black hair parted in the middle and curled around his forehead like mouse tails.

Slipchuck spat into the cuspidor on the floor. "Whiskey fer me. Near beer for my son."

Everybody in the vicinity looked at Slipchuck's "son." Nobody said a word. The bartender poured the drinks; Slipchuck flipped coins onto the bar. "Just stay where you are, barkeep, 'cause I'll be a-needin' a refill directly."

Slipchuck tossed the fiery liquid down his throat in one shot and slammed the glass on the bar. "That's some fine whiskey. Think I'm a-gonna like it here."

"The plan was make money and move on."

"Tomorrow we might be daid!"

Stone sipped the awful near beer, craved good whiskey, but was trying to stop drinking. Whores in brightly colored gowns sashayed by the bar. One dug painted fingernails into Stone's shoulder. "Buy me a drink?"

"You'll have to ask my banker." He pointed to Slipchuck.

She looked at Stone curiously as Slipchuck called the bartender. Her black-gloved hand held a black lace fan, her lips painted bloodred.

"Don't believe I've seen you in town before," she said. "What's yer name?"

Before Stone could answer, Slipchuck elbowed him to the side. "What's yer goin' rate, sweetheart?"

"Three dollars."

"How long?"

"Long as it takes."

"You got yourself a deal."

Stone grabbed Slipchuck's shoulder. "We're supposed to be looking for a hotel. We don't have much money. This is no time for the riding academy."

The whore looked coldly at Stone. "Mind yer own business."

"He *is* my business."

She rubbed against Slipchuck. "You gonna let this big galoot tell you what to do?"

Slipchuck gazed shamefacedly at Stone. "I always thinks better after I had a little nooky."

Stone sighed in defeat. His near beer smelled like horse urine. *Why can't I control my drinking?* He turned to the bartender and opened his mouth, but words froze in his throat. He remembered the time he awakened on a pile of horse manure. The bartender wiped his big gnarled hands on a towel.

"You got sarsaparilla?"

Stone heard a voice beside him. "How old're you, boy?"

Stone turned to a big strapping man with a bushy black beard and suspenders holding up his pants. "Old enough."

"That stuff's for the little 'uns. Have a whiskey on me. Bartender?"

The bartender filled the glass in front of Stone. Amber fluid twinkled in the light of coal-oil lamps. Blackbeard slapped Stone's shoulder. "Drink up, friend."

Stone stared at the whiskey laughing at him. He didn't feel like fighting a miner, but feared the devil's potion.

"I thought I said drink up!" The smile vanished slowly from the blackbeard's dusty visage. Stone stepped away from the bar. *Here I go again.* "I'm trying to quit drinking," he explained. "It's nothing personal. You want to sit down, I'll have supper with you, but if I start drinking, I'll end up dead."

The miner stared at him for a few moments, blinked, then lowered his hands. His murderous scowl became thoughtful. " 'Bout time I et, now that you mention it. There's an empty table over thar!"

Stone followed him across the congested floor. Croupiers spun roulette wheels, dice rolled over green cloth, cards shuffled. They came to an empty table in the middle of the hall, covered with empty bottles and glasses. The miner swept them to the side with his big arm and sat down.

"Name's Kevin McGeachy. I owns the Great Monarch Mine."

"John Stone, on my way to San Francisco."

"What the hell fer?"

"Joining my fiancée."

"Congratulations." McGeachy held out his hand, Stone shook it. "I been married a few times meself, but ain't no fun. There's one thing I larned about wimmin. They all nag. Larn it from their mommas at an early age." He lunged toward a waitress carrying a tray of drinks, she nearly spilled them onto the floor.

"Are you crazy!" she screamed. "What the hell's the matter with you!"

"Bottle of whiskey an' two steak platters with all the trimmin's." The waitress walked away in a huff. "That's the way to treat 'em. Don't take no back talk. You listen to me, you'll larn somethin'."

"How's the Great Monarch Mine doing?"

McGeachy wiped his nose with the back of his hand. "A few more feet, I'll hit the mother lode."

"I'm new in town. What's a good place to stay?"

" 'Pends on how much money you got."

"Not much."

"The tents on the far side of the railroad tracks is yer best bet. Fifty cents a night. Let me tell you somethin' about drinkin'. I know what it's like to wake up in jail for committin' a murder I don't even remember. But I won't drink sugar water. The trick is to pace yourself. I've been drinkin' since Monday, but I ain't fallin' on my face, am I? You have to be strong *inside*."

The waitress placed a bottle of whiskey and two glasses on the table. Stone stared at the amber fluid as if it were liquid dynamite. McGeachy said, "You weren't afraid of me, and I'm more dangerous than any bottle. The problem is you, not the whiskey. You got to wrestle the demon and cut his goldarned throat. Ain't good fer a man's spirit to be afraid of somethin'. It's only whiskey."

Stone thought: *Can I drink that stuff and not fall apart?*

"When you git dizzy," McGeachy said, "back off a little. Otherwise stay out of saloons."

Stone couldn't stay out of saloons. A man needs to talk with people. But he hesitated. McGeachy placed his hand on Stone's shoulder. "At a time like this, a man wants to be alone." He walked toward the back door of the Grand Palace.

Stone stared at the bottle.

ROCKY MOUNTAIN WHISKEY
Finest Blended Spirits

A little taste wouldn't hurt. *If I can't control my drinking, how can I control other parts of my life?* He uncorked the bottle. *If McGeachy can pace himself, why can't I? What the hell.*

The road to perdition was paved with what the hell's, but Stone wrapped his fingers around the glass. Slowly, as in a dream, he raised the liquid to his lips. His hand trembled. He was afraid, and set the glass down. Behind him, a table of miners pushed their chairs back. Hitching their gunbelts, buttoning their coats, they headed for the door. A newspaper lay atop one of the chairs. Stone reached for it. The *Lodestone Gazette,* three days old. The headline said: GOLD DISCOVERED ON RAPAHORN!

Front page covered with mining news. A listing of stock closing prices ran down the right gutter. The bankruptcy of a mining combine. A stagecoach holdup. Every story filled with breathless excitement. Ragged miners arriving with holes in their shoes were multimillionaires three days later, living luxuriously on the top floor of the Sheffield Hotel, while others blew their brains out after sinking everything they owned into a hole in the ground.

Stone turned to the next page. National news. The Fifteenth Amendment passed. A new warship christened in Newport News. Whaling industry in deep trouble. ROBERT E. LEE DIES.

Stone's heart stopped. He read the headline again. Choking sensation, confusion, the world crashed about him. Not Bobby Lee. A man like that couldn't die. The words floated before him.

Robert E. Lee, commanding general of the Army of Northern Virginia during the Rebellion, died today at his Lexington, Virginia home. He was 63. Considered by many the greatest general of the war, and a hero of the South, he'd been in failing health for the past several months, according to his family.

Stone felt nauseous. General Lee, noblest man in the world, gone. Gamblers tossed chips into the pot at the next table, a croupier spun his chuck-a-luck wheel.

"Round and round she goes, and where she stops, nobody knows!"

Stone looked at his glass of whiskey. *I'll make you feel better.* He reached toward it, saw General Lee's war weary face. Stone pushed the glass of whiskey farther away and returned his eyes to the news article.

Bobby Lee spent the last years of his life as president of Washington College in Virginia. When he assumed the position at the close of the war, the school had forty students and four professors. The hero of the Confederacy chose to educate the young, while Grant consorted with multimillionaires and waltzed through the White House.

Stone remembered Bobby Lee on his white horse, trooping the line, splendid in the saddle, like an old Roman god. Solid, steady, brilliant, unswerving, a man of honor to the core. Not even his worst enemies said anything bad about his character. He gave everything to the Confederacy, the war shortened his life, he didn't even believe in slavery. Bobby Lee freed most of his Negroes before the war, but had to defend the Southland against the armies of the North.

Stone served under Jeb Stuart, and many thought Gettysburg was lost because of old Jeb's wild antics.

The cavalry was General Lee's eyes and ears, but instead of reconnaissance, Jeb led his command in a wild spree through rural Pennsylvania, tore up railroad tracks, communication lines, burned supplies, lived off the land, great fun and high adventure for men barely out of their teens, but General Lee was defeated at Gettysburg due to lack of intelligence information. The Confederate Army was never the same again, thanks to good old Jeb.

General Lee never scolded Jeb. But the cavalry let General Lee down. Maybe that's why Jeb got killed at Yellow Tavern. He attacked a numerically superior Yankee force, and got shot.

Had he taken the chance to make it up to General Lee?

Stone met the general personally in 1864, after Bobby Lee assigned one of Wade Hampton's brigades to Fitzhugh Lee, the general's nephew. Wade Hampton rode to General Lee's headquarters with several officers to protest the move. The general was camped in a wilderness, weather damp and cold. Hampton introduced his staff, and young Captain Stone shook General Lee's rough old hand. "Keep up the good work," the general said. Then he and Wade Hampton retired to the commanding officer's private office.

Stone and the others waited outside, the walls of a tent thin, Hampton stated his case in low tones. Then they heard the slightly lower voice of Bobby Lee. "General Hampton, I expect you to follow orders. If you cannot, I would not care if you went back to South Carolina with your whole division."

Wade Hampton was pale with humiliation when he left the tent, but Bobby Lee had no patience with petty jealousy. He was fighting a war, wrong decisions cost lives, heavy burdens for a man in his fifties. On top of everything else, he'd been sick at Gettysburg.

A week never passed when Stone didn't run Gettysburg through his mind at least once. Thousands of men on horseback hacking each other with cavalry swords. Horror without parallel in his life, blood ran in rivulets on the ground. He fought in mad frenzy. Wade Hampton caught a saber on the skull and nearly died.

They let General Lee down. Stone would rather die, if he could turn it around. General Lee lost everything, including his home in Arlington, in a war he never wanted.

Wade Hampton tried to buy the general's good name after the war, offering the presidency of an insurance company. Nobody south of the Mason-Dixon Line would refuse Bobby Lee's life insurance. Instead, the old soldier turned Washington College into the South's finest school. God didn't make many men like Bobby Lee. The former captain of cavalry wiped a tear from his eye with the back of his hand.

A woman in pink tights and black mesh stockings dropped onto his lap. She had black hair and large brown eyes with long lashes.

"I'm Annie Mae. New in town?"

It took Stone a few moments to return from Gettysburg. "Just arrived. Looking for a job. Know of anything?"

"Always need experienced bartenders here. Talk to the boss."

"Who is he?"

"Belle McGuinness. Her office is in back. You ever been a bartender before?"

"Just pour whiskey into the glass, right?"

She became shy, a little girl wearing her mother's cosmetics, though she was old enough to be a mother herself. She slid off his lap and dropped onto the chair beside him. "Who the hell are you?"

Stone told her his name.

"Somethin' weird about you. You wanted for anythin'?"

"Not that I know of."

"You remind me of a feller I knew once who been in jail. You got the mad-dog look in yer eyes."

"What's Belle McGuinness like?"

"Don't ever cross her."

He headed for the rear of the saloon, asked a bartender where Belle McGuinness was.

"Foller yer nose down the hall."

Stone entered the corridor. The door said MAIN OFFICE. He removed his hat, wished he shaved that morning.

A scholarly looking man sat at a desk, while a gorilla in a suit read the *Lodestone Gazette* on a chair near the window.

"Whataya want?" asked the scholar.

"Belle McGuinness. I heard she's looking for a bartender."

"Where'd you work before?"

Stone pulled a saloon out of his memory. "The Last Chance in San Antone."

The scholar walked to a door at the rear of the office. Stone looked at the gorilla. "What's your job?"

The gorilla pointed to his mouth and made inarticulate sounds, deaf and mute. The scholar returned to the office. "Boss lady'll see you now."

Stone walked to the back room. A woman with blond hair piled high on her head sat behind the desk. She wore substantial cosmetics, black birthmark on her chin, pretty but hard-looking, maybe thirty-eight. "Have a seat."

Stone dropped onto a leather upholstered chair. "Miss McGuinness, I . . ."

She interrupted. "What d'you know 'bout tendin' bar?"

"Spent a lot of time in saloons. Know what makes a good bartender. Give 'em a good pour, don't forget to collect the money."

She was bold and brassy, all business. "Miners spend a few months in the hills, when they hit town, go loco. You got to be able to handle 'em. I pay ten dollars a week, plus yer meals. You can start tonight if you want, but understand one thing. Get caught stealin' from me, you're a dead man." She paused to let it sink it.

The scholar led Stone to the main room of the saloon. A group of dancers in tights kicked their heels, Annie Mae on the end. She blew a kiss to Stone as he followed the scholar behind a bar.

"Got some help for you fellers," the scholar said to two men working feverishly. "Move on down."

The scholar tossed Stone an apron, showed him glasses, whiskey bottles, beer keg, and near beer keg. "Fer the sissies and pantywaists what don't like the real stuff." He slapped Stone on the shoulder. "It's all yours."

The scholar walked away from the bar. Stone hung his old Confederate cavalry hat on a peg. Time to get acquainted with his fellow bartenders, but somebody hollered: "Whiskey!"

Stone turned to two bleary eyes in a body covered with dirt. The man looked like he just crawled out of a hole in the ground. Stone dropped a glass in front of him and filled it.

"Barkeep!"

He ran to another man. Three miners asked for a bottle of whiskey. Stone took money, made change, ran back and forth behind the bar, spurs clanging.

Customers were two or three deep at the bar. A woman shrieked as somebody pinched her bottom. A man with a feather in his derby roared like a lion. The band barely could be heard above the din, Stone placed a mug of beer in front of a customer, who snarled: "I said whiskey, not beer!"

The customer smacked the mug with the back of his hand, it flew at Stone, he tried to dodge, spilled over the front of his apron. His first instinct was punch him in the mouth, but he needed the job.

"Yes, sir," he said with a forced smile as he filled the glass.

A slender bony figure arose at the far end of the bar. Stone walked toward Slipchuck, eyes dazed, hat crooked on his head.

"Whiskey," Slipchuck said, not recognizing his pardner.

Stone poured the glass. "Fifty cents."

Slipchuck reached into his pocket.

"Spend it on whiskey," Stone said, "you'll be sleeping in an alley."

"Can't stand a bartender who preaches," Slipchuck replied. "I asked you fer a glass of whiskey, that's all I want it to be." Slipchuck looked into Stone's blue eyes, trying to intimidate him. "Johnny! What the hell you doin' there!"

"Just got hired."

"Bartender!" shouted the man who threw the beer at Stone.

Stone tried to smile. "What can I get you, sir?"

"I ain't figgered it out yet." He grabbed the front of Stone's shirt in his fist. "I don't like you."

The miner swung at Stone's head. Stone blocked it and ripped a solid left hook to the miner's face. The miner staggered backward and landed on his back, eyes closed, left leg shaking uncontrollably.

"Whiskey!"

Stone ran toward the customer. Everybody was calling him. He shifted around, filled glasses, took money, poured three glasses of whiskey for three gamblers in slick suits and neatly clipped mustaches.

"How's about one on the house?" Slipchuck asked, pushing his glass forward. Stone poured the drink.

"Bartender!"

Stone ran toward the voice of the miner he'd punched. Blood oozed from his split lip, he aimed a gun at Stone. "You son of a bitch—say yer prayers!"

Everybody in the vicinity sucked wind. A space opened on both sides of the miner. Stone stared down the barrel of a gun for the second time that day. If he could distract him . . .

A truncheon came crashing onto the miner's head. The miner's eyes rolled white, he dropped out of sight on the other side of the bar. Standing behind him was a powerfully built man. "No gunplay in the saloon."

Two men stepped out of the crowd, grabbed the miner by his arms and legs, carried him toward the back door. The miner's head hung back lifelessly, blood dripped out of his nose and ears.

Gail Petigru sat with her older sister, Mrs. Patricia Madden, in the dining room of the latter's two-story home on Hawthorne Street. Four tapered wax candles illuminated a roast turkey carved by the Maddens' Negro maid, Ethel.

"Sorry Bart can't join us," said Patricia, who'd gained twenty-five pounds since her marriage. "He often has to work late. He has many responsibilities."

"I'm looking forward to meeting him," Gail replied.

"He can be brusque at times, so don't be offended. As I said, he's a busy man."

Gail looked at a painting above the fireplace of President Grant as a three-starred general, her sister's home furnished like the finest in Bangor, her brother-in-law obviously a wealthy man.

"Married life's not all it's made out to be," Patricia said sadly as she buttered a biscuit. "Don't expect too much from a man. Love changes just as people change."

Gail touched her sister's hand. "I'm sorry . . ."

"Nothing different from any other marriage. Can't always be like the first few weeks. Do you have a beau?"

"Saw an interesting man on the train today. Much older than I, a former Confederate cavalry officer, but something sweet about him."

"What does he do for a living?"

"Said he was a cowboy."

"How drunk was he?"

"Didn't seem drunk at all."

"Unusual for a cowboy, but I don't suppose they're bad as miners. Miners are filthy, crazy, cut your throat for a dime. Did your Confederate charmer continue on to Denver?"

"He's in town."

"You'll have to invite him to supper with us one night."

"I don't know where he lives. All his money was stolen in the holdup. Said he'd find a job."

"Maybe Bart could get him something. Was he educated?"

"A college man, but wouldn't work in a bank. Doesn't like to shave."

"Is he good-looking?"

"He's been in some fights recently."

"Maybe you try for something a little better?"

"I'll probably never see him again. What time will Bart get home?"

"Sometimes he doesn't come home at all. Bart says there's ten times the activity here than in an ordinary town. I've been married three years, and all I can tell you is this: Men are fascinated with us, until they get us. Then they want us to be maids and mothers, and leave them alone."

Belle McGuinness sat in her office, cheroot in hand, studying the ledger on her desk. His sharp eyes roved up and down the columns, reading numbers the way another person reads a novel. The Grand Palace was healthy. Money rolled in night after night. She was in the right place for once in her life. If she could keep it up a few more years, she'd be rich.

Belle grew up poor and ragged, her mother a prostitute, nobody knew who her father was. She became a prostitute at twelve, a drunken farmer nearly beat her to death at thirteen. When fourteen, a soldier tried to jam his knife into her. She'd been in many cat fights with other women; a scar on her cheek was camouflaged with rouge. Her finishing schools were whorehouses. She learned to be cold and tough. You can't trust anybody. She carried a derringer in her garter.

Bart Madden, Patricia's husband, entered her office, wearing a dark blue business suit with long frock coat and wide striped cravat.

"What're *you* doin' here?" Belle asked. "Ruin your reputation, you git seen with me!"

"Do you mind?" He kissed her cheek. "I've missed you." He had dark saturnine features, straight nose, receding hairline.

She pushed him away. "Be careful you don't git powder on yer coat. Yer wife'll see it an' beat the shit out of you." Belle threw back her head and laughed.

Madden's face reddened. "Don't worry about my wife. I can handle her."

"Then why do we sneak around like we're doin' somethin' wrong?"

"Bank presidents can't leave their wives for other women. Doesn't look right in the banking community. Give me another year."

"Give you all the time you want, darlin'. Just remember, momma don't like to be alone."

He grabbed her shoulders. "My bank paid for every stick of wood in this building, every glass behind the bar, every thread on your back! You make a fool out of me, you'll be sorry!"

"You 'spect me to act like your wife," Belle said, "but you've got a legal wife, remember? Till you put that ring on my finger, you got no call to tell me how to live."

"If you loved me, seems you could wait." He wrapped his arms around her. "When the bank is on a more solid footing, I'll divorce my wife and marry you, I promise."

"No you won't. You're ashamed of me, because everybody in this town knows I was a whore."

"When my investments pay off, I could marry a nigger and get away with it. You'll be the queen of Lodestone when I'm finished with you."

"I'm queen of Lodestone now. Don't need you for that. I want a man who'll stand by me."

"That's me. I'll do it."

"Till you put that ring on my finger, I'm a free woman. You want to foreclose on the Grand Palace, I'll git my finances elsewhere. Even a fool can see this place is a gold mine."

He tried to keep smiling. What could he do to bring her into line? Hit a soft spot. "I always wanted somebody to have faith in me, believe in me, and trust me. If I say I'll marry you in a year, why can't you accept it?"

"If every man married me who said he would, I'd have more husbands than the King of Araby has wives. Like I said, till you give me a ring, I'm a-keepin' my eyes open."

Stone ran back and forth behind the bar. One drunkard after another. *Keep pouring. Wash glasses every chance you get. Give the right change.* Didn't know where he'd sleep that night, shirt soaked with sweat, apron covered with spilled everything.

"Where's that goddamn stupid bartender!"

A miner with a leather slouch hat stood before him, picking his teeth with a knife. "Bottle of booze."

Stone lifted it out of the case and set it before him. "Four dollars."

The miner dropped a five-dollar coin on the counter. Stone took it to the cashbox, retrieved one dollar, tossed it to the miner.

"I gave you a twenty-dollar gold eagle! You're a dirty cheatin' crook! I might be drunk, but I'm not that drunk." The miner smashed the bottle over the bar and held the lethal jagged edge in his fist.

Stone took a step back and waited for the timely arrival of the man with the truncheon, but he didn't come. The miner climbed on top of the bar.

"Go git 'im, Ned!" goaded a miner nearby.

Stone didn't dare shoot him in a town with a police department. "You'd better climb down. Check your money, you'll see I'm right."

The miner snarled, the bottle's edge glittering in the lamplight. He crouched, ready to jump on Stone, who drew a Colt and fired. The broken bottle shattered in Ned's hand. He stared at the tiny fragment remaining. Truth dawned on him. He made a self-conscious half smile, shrugged, lowered himself to the ground.

"That was some pretty fancy shootin'!" said a clean-shaven miner. "Who the hell're you?"

Stone holstered his gun, concerned both his Colts'd get rusty behind the bar, liquids splashing constantly, floor slippery, a man could break his neck, worse job he'd ever had.

"What does a man have to do to get a drink around here!"

Stone carried whiskey to a gambler in a white shirt and red cravat. Then he drew a mug of beer for a man who looked like the local schoolteacher. A miner passed out on the bar, cheek lying in a puddle of spit. Stone placed his hand on the miner's head and shook him. "Time to go home."

The miner didn't budge. Another customer pulled the drunkard out of the way and let him fall to the floor.

Stone filled the new customer's glass. A month as a bartender before he could leave for San Francisco, wasn't sure he could make it. *Maybe I can find a better job.*

Bart Madden walked toward the best neighborhood in Lodestone, hands shoved into his pockets, mind still at the Grand Palace.

He didn't know what to do about Belle, because he'd fallen in love with her. But everyone knew what she was. He'd be ostracized. A banker had to be respectable, but Belle wanted a ring on her finger.

Madden had a headache. *Too much on my mind.* Some said the mines were petering out. The maid took his hat and cane. His wife sat in the living room with a young woman who bore the Petigru family resemblance.

"My sister, Gail."

A choice morsel, he thought as he took her hand. "Heard you had a bad trip."

"I was robbed at gunpoint."

"Welcome to the frontier." He sat on an upholstered red velvet chair in front of the fireplace. The maid brought a glass of whiskey. "Patricia'll give you the grand tour tomorrow. Watch out for drunks."

The clock on the mantel said ten o'clock. "I'm awfully tired," Gail said. "Do you mind if I turn in early?"

Patricia escorted her upstairs. They entered the guest bedroom. Patricia frowned as she pulled down the bedspread.

"Are you all right?" Gail asked.

"Just a little distracted. Sleep well."

Patricia descended the stairs. Bart sat in his office, looking at documents. Patricia stood before the desk. "How dare you disgrace me in front of my sister!"

"I say something wrong?"

"You can smell that woman's cheap perfume all over the house. Do you think I don't know?"

"Know what?"

"Everything about you and Belle McGuinness! I don't care what you do with her, but just don't bring her into my house!"

She stormed out of the office. *How does she know?* He bit his cigar. If she left him now, bad for business. He found her in the kitchen, taking a glass of water from the maid. "Ethel, would you leave us alone for a moment, please?"

The maid retreated. "It's not what you think," Madden said to Patricia. "You know how evil gossip is."

"Cheap perfume isn't gossip. I'm sure my sister noticed it."

"I had a drink, so what? I have to mix with the populace. That's how I drum up business for the bank. They might look like drunken prospectors to you, but some are worth millions."

"They wear cheap perfume?" Patricia asked sarcastically.

"Wherever miners go, you find women. I have to mix with the people."

"Mix with whoever you want. Rut with hogs if you want. But keep them out of this house!"

Gail undressed in front of the mirror. She was five-two, smooth creamy skin, full of life and hope, but something missing.

She knew what it was. When would he come along? Her sister was already an old lady at twenty-five. Gail dropped a nightgown over her head, blew out the lamp, crawled beneath the covers.

Flannel sheets and wool blankets radiated her body warmth. She cuddled against the pillow and thought of her sister's marriage. Did all men tire of women after getting what they wanted?

She thought of the ex-cavalry officer, his steely reserve. *Wonder where he's sleeping right now?*

3

THE SINGER IN the black suit bowed, spangles flashing in the lamplight. The band took a break. John Stone's jaw hung with fatigue as he looked at empty glasses lined up on the bar.

"Hey, bartender!"

Everybody wanted him. *What'm I doing here?* Annie Mae stood at the end of the bar and rapped her knuckles. "Whiskey!"

Stone poured, dashed to the cash box, returned with change. A miner with a beard to his chest stood next to her. "Buy you a drink?"

"Got one," she replied, and looked the other way.

"Don't turn yer back on me!" He grabbed her shoulder and spun her around.

"Take yer hands off'n me!"

He grinned, one tooth missing on top. "What if'n I don't!"

"You're hurtin' me!"

"Don't git uppity with me, you goddamned whore!"

He smacked her across the face with the back of his hand. She went flying across the floor.

The man with the truncheon maneuvered in front of the miner. "You'd better settle down, mister."

"Put that thing away," the miner replied, "or I'll shove it up yer ass."

The truncheon swung at the miner's head, but the miner reached up and grabbed the bouncer's wrist, then kicked between his legs. The bouncer hunched over and dropped moaning to the floor.

The miner pulled his blade and turned to Annie Mae, who pressed her back against the wall, trying to get away from him. "So you don't like Jack, eh? When I finish with you, no man'll ever look at you again!"

Annie Mae opened her mouth and screamed. She looked like a terrified child wearing her mother's makeup. Jack drew lips over his teeth. She covered her face with her fingers and hollered.

A shadow fell over her. "Leave her alone," said John Stone.

Jack saw guns in his hands. "You'd better put them pea-shooters away, 'cause I ain't afraid of you."

"One move toward her, you're a dead man."

Jack stared down the gun barrels. Then he looked into John Stone's eyes. Bluffing? Jack pushed the knife into his scabbard. "Maybe some other time."

Annie Mae sobbed. Stone placed his arm around her shoulders and led her toward the back door.

"Watch out!"

Jack lunged toward Stone, knife in hand. Stone slammed his palm on Jack's wrist, the blade sliced across Stone's thigh. Stone took one step to the side and threw a stiff uppercut.

It caught Jack coming in. Stone darted to the side as Jack's momentum carried him forward. The miner crashed into the wall, stunned for a few moments. When his head cleared, John Stone stood in front of him, left pant leg red with blood.

"You best get out of here while you can still walk," Stone said.

"And don't ever come back again!" Everyone turned to Belle McGuinness, standing at the edge of the crowd, wearing a red satin gown.

Jack laughed, brandishing his bloody knife. "You want me to leave, you'll have to throw me out."

Stone thought of shooting him. Where were the police? "You don't get out of here on your own steam, I'll put you through the window."

"Like to see you try."

Jack waved the blade of his knife from side to side and dropped into his knifefighter's crouch. "I'll cut you from hell to breakfast."

The crowd swarmed around. Stone wondered whether to pull his gun. Suddenly Jack thrust his knife toward the front of Stone's shirt. Stone grabbed Jack's wrist with his left hand, rammed his forearm against Jack's elbow. A sickening *crack,* Jack bellowed in pain. Stone cracked him in the face. The miner sailed through the air, landed on a table, slid to the floor. Stone lifted him by the belt and carried him toward the nearest door. It opened, and two uniformed deputies entered the Grand Palace, flanking a man with a bushy mustache, wearing a badge on the lapel of his suit.

The marshal looked Stone over. "What's your name?"

They heard Belle's voice. "He's one of my bartenders. The miner cut him."

The marshal looked at Stone's leg. Stone saw a strange scimitar scar at the corner of his eye.

"Watch yer step," the marshal said gruffly to Stone in a voice that sounded familiar.

"Drinks on the house!" shouted Belle.

Two deputies picked up the unconscious miner and carried him toward the door. Stone watched the peace officers disappear into the crowd. "What's the marshal's name?" he asked Belle.

"Bill Kincaid. C'mon back to my office. I'll look at that leg."

He followed her through the crowd. Belle was full-bodied, medium height, an armful for any man. Miners tipped their hats as she passed. The lamp in her office had gone out.

"Got a match?" she asked.

She lifted the chimney, he set the wick aflame, she aware of muscles straining the fabric of his shirt. His profile, against the lamplight, pleased her eye. She replaced the chimney and adjusted the wheel.

"What you say your name was?"

"John Stone."

"Lie down on the sofa. You'll have to take your pants off." She threw a towel. He stepped behind her dressing screen. "Shy?" she asked sarcastically. "I seen little boys before."

Blood coagulated on the wound. He wrapped the towel around his waist and limped toward the sofa. Belle rolled up the sleeves of her blouse.

"Bartenders usually dive 'neath the bar at the first sign of trouble," she said. "Why'd you take on Jack?"

"What happened to your bouncer?"

"You want his job? Pays five more dollars a week than you're gittin' now."

"When do I start?"

"Never figgered you fer a bartender."

She placed the basin beside him and knelt, his leg covered with golden hair. The wound was a three-inch slash with ragged edges. She rinsed the washcloth, wrung it out, patted his wound gently. Long ago she learned to hide feelings behind an impenetrable wall. She covered the bloody line with a bandage. "Don't know how yer pants'll fit over this."

"What you know about Marshal Kincaid?"

"Best marshal money can buy."

"Where'd he come from?"

"Here in Lodestone, we generally don't ask people where they come from."

"He arrive alone?"

"What's Marshal Kincaid to you?"

"Always a good idea to know who the lawman is."

"He's got sand. That's all you've got to know. Some lawmen hide when trouble starts, but not Bill Kincaid. He keeps the peace pretty damn good in this town."

"How about outside town?"

"Roads ain't safe, if that's what you mean. Lots of holdups. You 'spect that in gold country. Kincaid can't be everywheres, but he catches crooks. We had a hangin' here two weeks ago. You stick around, you'll prob'ly see the next one."

Marshal Kincaid puffed his corncob pipe and looked out the window of his office. Drunks staggered over the sidewalks, a wagonful of miners passed in the street. The stamp mill pounded incessantly in the distance.

He thought about John Stone. Rob a man in the afternoon, come face-to-face with him that night. Marshal Kincaid dug dottle from the bowl of his pipe with a pocketknife, then blew through the stem. A stream of tobacco juice squirted into the air.

He put on his hat and looked in the mirror. His belly hung over his belt, he had jowls. Retire in Mexico in a few more years. Can't let an odd coincidence spoil everything.

He walked out the door. Across the street, a group of miners entered the Grubstake Saloon. On the corner, a deputy twirled his club beside a streetlamp. "Find Tommy Moran, tell him to meet me behind the Lodestone Savings Bank in a half hour."

Stone limped to an empty table in a dark corner, sat on a chair, blew out the candle. The corner plunged into darkness. He had a lot to think about, Belle McGuinness uppermost in his mind. A strange woman, beautiful, hard as nails, but sensitive beneath her carefully manufactured exterior. Probably didn't even know she was acting most of the time.

A few tables away, a miner jumped into the air and screamed. Then he scooped up a big pile of chips, cackling like a maniac. Men hollered at each other angrily near the bar.

A figure in a white suit sat beside him. "Looks like you got a promotion," Slipchuck said. "You find out if she had somethin' fer me?"

"Didn't think of it, but we'll set it straight right now."

Stone walked back to Belle's office. Slipchuck hitched up his pants, hoping to make a good impression on the boss lady.

"John Stone and a friend of his'n to see you, Miss Belle. You too busy to see 'em?"

"Send 'em in."

John Stone entered, accompanied by a filthy little old man. "This is my pardner, Mr. Slipchuck."

Slipchuck removed his dirty hat and made an elaborate bow.

"I know he doesn't look like much," Stone said, "but he saved my life more'n once. Not afraid of anything. You need another bouncer, he's your man."

Belle raised the back of her hand to her mouth and laughed. Slipchuck blushed to the roots of his gray hair. He yanked out his trusty Colt and aimed at her. "No woman makes fun of me an' gits away with it!"

Stone whacked Slipchuck's gun downward, Slipchuck pulled the trigger, the bullet crashed into the floorboards. A cloud of acrid gunsmoke filled the office.

Slipchuck took a stance like a fighting cock. They were the strangest duo Belle had ever seen. How could they be pardners? John Stone clearly cared for the old man.

"Have a seat," she said, holding out her box of cheroots.

"Don't mind if'n I do," Slipchuck replied.

He selected one and lit it with a match. So did Stone. Their heads disappeared in a vast cloud of blue smoke. Belle leaned toward Slipchuck. "I can tell a gentleman when I see one. Bouncer ain't no job fer you. How'd you like to work on the second floor with the girls?"

"With the girls?" Slipchuck asked in disbelief.

"Sweep the corridors, keep the stoves goin'. Fix anythin' that might go wrong."

John Stone was indignant. "You can't give my pardner a janitor job. Anybody can see he deserves better than that."

Slipchuck held up his hand. "Hold on, Johnny. Lemme speak fer meself." He turned to Belle. "You say I'll be on the second floor where the gals live."

"Yer job is take care of 'em," she replied.

"You got yerself a deal!" Slipchuck slammed the heel of his fist upon her desk.

Belle turned to John Stone. "Stop at my room when you get off work tonight. Somethin' I want to talk to you about."

Marshal Kincaid sat on the ground, puffing his corncob pipe, his back leaned against the rear wall of the bank. A thin sliver of curved moon hung on the horizon. He felt nostalgic for the open range. Long ago he'd been a cowboy.

Footstep in the alley, Kincaid drew his gun and melted into the shadows. The figure of a man emerged from the night. Moonlight silhouetted his profile.

"Kincaid?"

"Over here."

Tommy Moran walked toward him, head cocked to the side, sturdily built, black hair, black mustache. "What you got fer me, Marshal?"

"His name's John Stone. He's at the Grand Palace. Yer goin' rate is sixty dollars?"

"Half in advance."

Marshal Kincaid pulled a handful of coins out of his pocket. "How soon can you do it?"

"Right now, if you want."

Slipchuck pushed his broom down the main corridor of the second floor. He'd been over the same territory ten times already, but that didn't stop him. Usually he had to pay, get it over with, get out. Never before had he taken time to observe the activity. A pudgy, dew-eyed whore wearing a thin chemise approached from the far end of the corridor. *A man lives long enough, all his dreams come true.*

Tommy Moran entered the Grand Palace, didn't step out of the backlight. He was ready, the swagger and confidence of a gunfighter as he approached the bar.

"Whiskey."

The bartender filled a glass. Moran spilled a few drops on his tongue for good luck. He had a description of John Stone. Before shooting his quarry, liked to study him, understand his quirks. Made it more interesting.

A whore with long red hair down her back approached and wrapped one arm around his shoulder. "Wanna come upstairs?"

"I'm lookin' for John Stone. Know where he is?"

"The corner over there."

Moran saw only darkness. "I can't see him."

She pinched his nose. "But he can see you."

Stone noticed Moran and the whore, two faces in a sea of humanity drinking, playing cards, shooting dice, reading newspapers, arguing. A mangy spotted dog strolled toward Stone, bone clamped in his jaws. A miner booted his tail, the dog scurried away.

A miner danced a jig atop a table, while a circle of onlookers clapped. A glass of beer flew through the air. A dude with a black mustache strolled along the aisle. Their eyes met. Tommy Moran made his way back to the bar. "Whiskey."

A tiny dot of red floated in the shadows, as Stone smoked a cigarette. He was unaware of Moran's scrutiny, the gunfighter just another customer. Stone was lost in thoughts of bygone days with the golden girl he was supposed to marry.

He remembered the night he proposed. They'd gone for a walk in the woods. He was only fourteen, and she one year younger. Beside a spring, he perched on one knee and asked her to be his wife when they were older. She said yes, and they drank the blood of the forest from the same cup.

The band struck up a jig. Tommy Moran rolled a cigarette, his brow furrowed. Something strangely familiar about John Stone. Had they met before? Maybe he just looked like somebody. *Either way, it doesn't matter. He's going to die right now.*

Slipchuck climbed the stairs affixed to the rear of the Grand Palace, a load of firewood in his arms. He opened the door, pulled back a curtain with his leg, lowered the wood to the floor. Bark and a worm remained on his sleeves. He brushed them off and leaned against the wall.

"I'm a-gittin' too old fer this shit."

He heard footsteps, snapped to attention. A whore pulled the curtain aside. "Thought you'd be a-hidin' back here, you old buzzard. Me stove's nearly out. Fix it while I go downstairs. Room twenty-five."

He followed her down the hall, watching the sway of her shapely hips beneath her pink silk dress. He came to her room, smelled her perfume. A Negro maid put fresh sheets on the bed.

"Gittin' cold in here," she said. "Git the fire goin', old man."

"Ain't that old."

He opened the door of the potbellied stove, stirred the ashes, threw in a few sticks of wood. The maid departed. Every customer got clean sheets, one of the establishment's main selling points.

Slipchuck, alone in a whore's boudoir, didn't have to hurry for a change. He clasped hands behind his back and looked around philosophically. The headboard of the bed was painted white, brass ornaments on the bedposts. Slipchuck placed his hand on the mattress, calculated the bounce. Not bad at all.

A table covered with cosmetics across the room. He held a bottle of perfume to the lamplight. Paints and rouge. The things they do.

He opened her closet. Two frilly dresses, thick wool coat, blouses and skirts, silk fabric, baubles, glitter, black mesh stockings, and lace underwear. Drive a man crazy.

A fight broke out in the middle of the bar. John Stone hoped it'd end by itself. A crowd formed, people shouted, a bottle crashed to the floor.

John Stone drew himself to his full height. No rest for the wicked. He put on his old Confederate cavalry hat and strolled toward the commotion. At its center, two filthy miners held knives in their hands.

Stone stepped between them. "You want to kill each other, do it outside."

"Out of the way," said one of them, wearing a new yellow shirt. "If I have to cut you to git to him, don't make a shit to me."

Stone snapped both guns on him so fast his hands blurred. "Try it."

Yellow shirt grimaced. "You wouldn't dare."

Men dived behind the bar. Another contingent ran at the door. Some jumped out windows. A few fell behind table barricades. Stone stepped backward and faced both miners. "I said get out."

"You wouldn't dare shoot me," yellow shirt said.

Stone pulled the trigger in his right hand. A shot rang out, yellow shirt felt something tug his hat. He took it off, saw a bullet hole in the crown.

"Next one goes between your eyes."

The miners looked at each other sheepishly. Eyes peered over the bar and through windows. "You'd better never let me catch you alone in a dark alley," said the miner to Stone, " 'cause I'll cut yer fuckin' throat."

Stone squeezed his trigger, the knife flew out of the miner's grip. "You ever see me again, you'd better walk the other way." He turned to yellow shirt. "That goes for you too."

"How about me?" Tommy Moran stood at the edge of the crowd, twirling his gun around his forefinger. He threw the weapon into the air and caught it behind his back, then spun it a few times and let it fall into the holster. "If they want to fight, let 'em fight."

"They can fight outside."

"I say let 'em fight here."

"You don't like the way I run this saloon, take it away from me."

Moran expected to brace Stone, but Stone turned it around. The ex-West Pointer raised his palms above his gun grips. Moran was confused. Stone stepped toward him, Confederate cavalry hat slanted low over his eyes. Moran flashed on Antietam. He stared at Stone in disbelief. It couldn't be!

"You going to fight?" Stone asked.

Moran tried to smile. But he'd met John Stone before. Moran cleared his throat. "They say only a fool mixes in other people's fights."

He turned away. Stone wondered why he backed off so suddenly. Customers gawked over the bar.

"Moran was skeered of him," somebody said.

Moran heard the remark, his blood ran hot. But he couldn't shoot John Stone.

"Thought Moran was tough," another man sneered.

Moran never backed down in his life. But he was bewildered, frightened, shaken to the marrow of his bones. He burst out the door and walked swiftly away, seeking a dark quiet spot where he could be alone and think it through.

Stone returned to his favorite table. The saloon refilled with customers. Little black balls spun around roulette highways. Gamblers and miners threw their money down. A whore shrieked with delight as a drunken miner hugged her tightly.

One moment he wanted to kill me, the next moment looked like the saloon fell on him. Why'd he back down?

Belle lay naked in her bathtub, steam curling from the surface of the sudsy water. Flames roared in the fireplace, a cheroot stuck beneath her teeth, she leaned backward and closed her eyes.

Heat permeated her flesh and bones. She sighed contentedly, and thought of John Stone. More muscles than he knew what to do with. But Bart Madden had money and power. A woman can get anything she wants, if she's smart.

Time, her worst enemy, skin not firm as five years ago, breasts didn't stand up quite as proudly. But she knew old whores who earned more than younger ones. All in the technique.

If you can't get a man one way, try another. John Stone would be a special treat after too many nights with the Bart Maddens of the world.

Beneath her harsh exterior, Belle McGuinness needed a man. But not everyone would do. John Stone was her type. They'd have a good time, and when it was over, go their separate ways. No point getting crazy over a man. None of them're worth it.

Tommy Moran bit his knuckles so hard they bled. He sat on his bed in the hotel room, remembering Antietam. He served in the Third Provisional Brigade under General George Crook, and was hit by a squadron of Confederate cavalry during the second day of fighting.

A Confederate officer's horse was shot out from underneath him only yards away, the officer thrown clear. The rebel commander drew his sword, shouted to his men, and charged on foot.

Moran knelt in a trench, aimed his rifle at the officer, and pulled the trigger. The cartridge didn't fire, and the Confederate officer continued his forward movement. Moran jumped to his feet, bayonet affixed to the end of his rifle. He took the stance for close combat.

The Confederate officer didn't stop. Moran thrust his rifle and bayonet toward him. The officer brought his saber down swiftly, whacking the rifle and bayonet out of the way. On the backswing, the officer crashed his sword into Moran's ribs.

Moran was hurled to the ground. He rolled onto his back and looked up through a sea of pain at the Confederate officer raising his sword for the coup de grace.

The Confederate officer gazed down, then muttered something Moran couldn't understand. The officer stepped over Moran's prostrate body and walked away. Moran passed out afterward, woke up three days later at a field hospital, surrounded by dead and dying.

But he survived. He lifted his shirt and looked at the scar across his lumpy ribs. Back at the saloon, when he took a close-up look at John Stone, he saw the Confederate officer who'd spared his life at Antietam so many years ago.

That's why he backed off. Couldn't kill the man who gave his life back. He didn't know what to do. Wherever he went, he might run into somebody who saw him turn yellow in Lodestone. *Could haunt me for the rest of my life.*

He was a gun for hire, but lived by a code. You don't shoot somebody who saved your life. He took thirty dollars out of his pocket, felt like Judas Iscariot. The coins burned his hand, he wanted to fling them away. Give the money back and get out of town. Make a new start someplace else. Killing people didn't make sense anymore. Whatever gave him the idea in the first place?

A portly man wearing a top hat and plaid vest approached John Stone's table. "I'm Edgar Faraday, publisher of the *Lodestone Gazette.* May I join you?" He sat, crossed his chubby legs, pulled a notepad from an inner pocket of his frock coat. "Thought I'd get the story from the horse's mouth, as it were. Your name's John Stone? Could you describe to me, in your own words, what happened tonight?"

"Don't have time."

"I was referring specifically to the incident with Tommy Moran. I understand you backed him down."

"You want the story, ask him."

Faraday wore thick round spectacles perched on his minuscule nose, his teeth stained with the tobacco he constantly chewed. The odor of alcoholic beverages emanated from his being. He cocked an eye and examined Stone carefully.

"You sound like an educated man. Where'd you go to school?"

"Long time ago."

"On the dodge?"

"Not yet."

"Not very friendly. Would you rather I put on the front page that the man who shot Tod Buckalew is in town?"

"Who told you that?"

"Hard to remember. Happened so long ago." Faraday winked.

"Every gun-crazy kid in town'll try to shoot me."

"Ever done newspaper work? I'll pay you ten dollars a week more than you're getting here."

"I'm getting sixty dollars a month," Stone lied.

"Seventy," said Faraday.

Wheels spun in Stone's mind. He wouldn't have to fight the Grand Palace Saloon every night. In a month, San Francisco. His best offer so far. "I'll need an advance, so I can get a hotel room."

Faraday tossed him a ten dollar gold coin. Stone lit the lamp and held the coin to the light. Faraday spit a brown stream of tobacco juice at the nearest cuspidor, missed by three inches. "You can start by writing the story of what happened here, and don't spare the details. I want to see every drop of blood. Glad to have you aboard. Put 'er there." They shook hands. "You go to West Point?"

Stone was surprised by his sudden question. Faraday chuckled. "A newspaperman develops a sharp eye after many years observing humanity. I can see your Confederate officer's campaign hat, and your confidence borders on arrogance. You're a West Pointer down on your luck, am I right?"

"A newspaperman sees everything." Stone removed the picture of Marie from his shirt pocket. "Ever run into this woman?"

Faraday adjusted his eyeglasses and held the picture up to the light. "Wish I met her. What's she to you?"

"I'm on my way to meet her in San Francisco. Guess she didn't stop off in Lodestone."

"Would've noticed if she had. Pretty gal."

A commotion broke out at the doors, the saloon invaded by women in high-necked black dresses, carrying signs:

REPENT DRUNKARDS
COME TO THE LORD

One was lifted by her cohorts onto a table. She raised her black-gloved fist in the air and shouted: "Children are starving tonight, because of drink! Women weep in hovels, because of drink! The Lord God calls on all drunkards to repent! Even the vilest of you can be forgiven if you repent! The kingdom of God is within you, saith the Lord God! Throw away that accursed whiskey and follow me! Dedicate yourself to the will of the Lord!"

A roar of approval arose from the throats of stern-faced women, armed with signs. WHISKEY IS THE DEVIL'S BREW.

They accosted miners, whores, and cardsharps. A tubby little old lady waddled toward Stone, her face pinched by years of bitterness and anger. "Drunkard!" she hollered at Stone. "You'll meet your death at the bar!"

Stone remembered something an old cowboy told him once. *If you git into an argument with a woman, grab yer hat and run.*

Stone plunged into the crowd. Another woman loomed up in front of him. "Repent!" She kicked him in the shins.

Edgar Faraday ran for cover. "I want the full story on my desk by nine in the morning, and don't leave out the details!"

A biddy hit Stone across the spine with a chair. "Deserter of babes! Violator of young maidens!"

Stone crawled on all fours toward the back door. A woman with a face like a prune dumped a pitcher of beer over his head. He jumped to his feet, joining a crowd of men fleeing in panic. The woman standing on the table waved her arms hysterically and shrieked: "You'll burn in hell forever, dirty rum-soaked pigs! The devil's got his hold on you, but Baby Jesus holds out His merciful hand! Accept His wonderful invitation! If you follow Jesus, He'll never let you down!"

A drunkard lying in a pool of vomit on the floor hollered in sobbing pain: "He let me down a hundred times! There ain't no Jesus! We're all alone here!"

She pointed her long finger at him. "Look at you up to your ears in filth! That's what happens to the man who trades his faith in the Lord for a bottle of cheap rotgut whiskey!"

A deep barreling woman's voice replied from the top of the stairs: "It's the best whiskey in the Rockies!" Belle stood resolutely in a white-and-red-striped satin dress, rifle in her hands.

The preacher woman glowered at her. "There she is, the whore of Babylon herself! The devil's seed! She's made widows and orphans! Sucked the blood of this community! Yet the Lord will forgive *even this woman* if she falls down and repents! Though her sins be as scarlet, they shall be white as snow!"

Belle pointed her rifle at the lady preacher. "You take their money and give 'em a two-bit sermon! I give 'em the best pour in town, the best steaks in the Rockies, and if Jesus came to Lodestone tomorrow, first spot he'd visit would be the Grand Palace!"

The lady preacher trembled with barely concealed rage. "Blasphemy! You'll boil in everlasting hell! Thou shalt not take the Lord's name in vain! She's the devil's bride, ladies and gentlemen! You know her past! She fornicated for pennies beside the railroad tracks when this town was founded! Filth and corruption are in her soul! Turn away from her, my friends! The Lord God calls to you from His holy tabernacle!"

Belle looked magnificent at the top of the stairs, her fabulous full figure illuminated by light from the nearby chandelier. The preacher lady, slender, no trace of cosmetics, not more than forty, her eyes ablaze with the deep conviction that God spoke to her.

"How can she sleep at night? Ladies and gentlemen, we've got to run her out of town! Send her forth into the wilderness! Let her lay with animals and snakes!"

"D'ruther lay with animals and snakes than with you! I'm a-gittin' sick of this goddamn circus! This is private property! Where's my bouncer?"

Her eyes roved the crowd, and fell on John Stone. "Throw her the hell out of here!"

Belle spun around and walked away. Stone hadn't time to tell her he was the new reporter for the *Lodestone Gazette*. They'd laugh if he ran from a woman. And such an unreasonable holier-than-thou crow she was too. She reminded Stone of a schoolmarm he had.

"Who is she?" Stone asked the miner standing beside him.

"Reverend Rebecca Hawkins, First Christian Assembly."

He walked toward her, and caught her eye. She pointed at him as he approached. "Do you see this man!" she screeched. "He's the Roman soldier who nailed Christ to the cross! You pay him, he'll use the strength God gave him against the people of God! He just does his duty like a soldier! He even wears an old soldier's hat! But we're not afraid of him, because we're the Christian soldiers of the Lord God Almighty!"

A solid phalanx of upright religious women formed before Rebecca Hawkins, arms crossed over their breasts. Stone stopped. How could he get through?

They advanced toward him. He couldn't fight an army of women! Run while you've got the chance. The women stepped closer, eyes narrowed with hate.

Something growled at his feet. He looked down and saw the mangy spotted hound who'd gnawed a bone earlier. The mutt glowered at the women, their turn to stop. The dog trudged forward, snarling deep in his throat. Long teeth flashed in the light of lanterns. The women made way for him, Stone followed toward the table where Reverend Hawkins stood, expression of fear growing on her face.

Stone grabbed her thin waist, she tried to kick him, he turned her on her side and carried her like a log toward the nearest door.

"You'll roast in the ovens of hell! They'll boil you in oil till the end of time! Imps will pull off your nose and ears! You'll be an abomination in the eyes of the Lord!"

A grateful miner opened the door. Stone carried her onto the front veranda of the Grand Palace and set her down. A few women made aggressive motions toward Stone, but the dog snarled. The preacher lady quivered with rage. "He's the devil's spawn!" she cried, pointing at Stone. "One day the devil will claim him!"

Marshal Kincaid felt an elbow in his ribs. "Somebody's at the door," his wife mumbled, half asleep. "Dig the dirt out'n yer ears, maybe you'd hear somethin'."

He opened his eyes. The sound of tapping came to his ears. "Whozzat?"

"One way to find out," his wife replied. "Get up off'n yer ass and go downstairs."

He rolled out of bed in his long johns, pulled on his pants, stepped into high-topped boots. Then he strapped on his six-gun. His wife returned to slumber, her rump like a mountain in the middle of the bed.

He descended the stairs. The door knocked again. He reached the main floor and paused, gun in hand. Tommy Moran stood before him, an agitated expression in his eyes.

"Brought your money back." Moran held the coins in his palm. "Couldn't do it."

"Why in hell not?"

"We met before," Moran said mysteriously.

"You and Stone?"

"Can't shoot him. Get somebody else."

Kincaid accepted the coins. "You'll never work for me again."

"My gun ain't for hire no more, so we're even. I'm be a-leavin' town tonight. Nice to know you."

Moran walked away. Kincaid dropped the coins into his pocket, closed the door. He climbed the stairs, thinking of what Moran said. The gunfighter looked like he'd seen a ghost.

Kincaid entered the bedroom. His wife rolled over and said, "Who was it?"

"Mistake."

She patted the mattress beside her. "Come to bed."

He reached for his gunbelt buckle, his hands froze. If Moran went round the bend, no telling what he might say. The whole house of cards could come tumbling down. Marshal Kincaid reached into the closet for a shirt. Some jobs a man has to do himself.

The dog followed Stone into the kitchen. A Negro with a mustache fried steaks and potatoes at the big stove. Stone reached into a tubful of meat and pulled out the biggest porterhouse he could find. He dropped it onto a plate. "This is for you," he said to the dog. He filled a bowl with water and set it beside the plate.

The saloon was half-full, the night winding down. A drunkard lay underneath a table. Another slept against a wall. Stone knew all about it, spent many nights in saloons.

He didn't feel better sober, but at least his head was clear. He didn't have to worry about walking into walls, or shooting himself by mistake. Sobriety provided a sense of security. He could handle anything.

Belle told him to stop by. He climbed the stairs. On the second floor, a lone figure kneeled before a door, peering through the keyhole. Slipchuck glanced guiltily at Stone, then pretended to be searching for something on the floor.

"Lost me hankie," Slipchuck said.

"Somebody catches you looking through keyholes, liable to put a bullet through your head."

Slipchuck held his finger in front of his lips and whispered, "What you doin' up here? Lookin' fer poontang?"

"Got to see the boss lady."

Slipchuck's eyes twinkled with mischief. "How come?"

"Business, I guess."

"All the wimmin's after you, Johnny boy. Wish I could be in yer boots."

Stone climbed to the third floor. Fatigue took the spring from his knees. He hoped the boss lady wouldn't keep him up too long. Not in the mood for a woman giving orders.

He came to the third floor, door straight ahead, brass rapper. He slammed it three times. Silence. Maybe gone to sleep. The door opened on a gorgeous Negro maid.

"Mr. Stone?" she asked. "Miss McGuinness is waiting for you in the parlor. Would you follow me, please?"

She led him through an anteroom and corridor, walls covered with gaudy oil paintings of landscapes, seascapes, nymphs, nude men and women frolicking in gardens. They came to an immense room with three sofas arranged around a fireplace filled with roaring logs. Belle sprawled on a sofa, wearing a black gown with low décolletage, cheroot in one hand, champagne glass in the other.

"Look who's here," she said in her husky voice. "Sit down and have some bubbly."

Above the fireplace hung an oil painting of George Washington chopping down the cherry tree. Lamps and candelabra burned on the mantel, four rifles mounted on a rack near the window, the head of a buffalo stared across the room at a painting of Napoleon leading the charge at Austerlitz.

Heat blasted from the fireplace. Stone loosed the bandanna around his neck. She lay resplendent beside him, silk gown revealing every curve of her body, including nipples and naval. She was practically naked. His right hand trembled.

An intoxicating perfume arose from her body. "I said, have some bubbly." She pointed to the bottle in the bucket.

"Don't drink," he replied.

"Little bubbly won't hurt you."

She raised herself to a sitting position, leaned toward him, poured champagne into his glass. He could see all the way to the deepest secrets of her bosom. Her perfume was devastating. She handed him the effervescent liquid. "Here's to the new manager of the Grand Palace Saloon. Pays a hundred dollars a month."

"To do what?"

"You'll run the saloon operation. I got too many other things to do."

"Told Edgar Faraday I'd work for him at the *Lodestone Gazette*."

"What's he payin'?"

"Seventy dollars a month."

"Why work fer less? Let's drink on it."

Stone was about to say: *I don't drink,* but comes a point where a man has to stop making excuses. *Champagne is pisswater compared to what I used to drink.* The rims of their glasses clicked. Her perfume swept over him, clouding his senses, her eyes deep pools of immeasurable delights. She touched the tip of her tongue to the rim of her glass, her eyes mocked him.

"Nothin' like bubbly to end the day."

Champagne tickled the roof of his mouth and glided down his throat, subtle as a woman. Firelight flickered on her face. An artery throbbed in his throat. She was there for him, round, soft, voluptuous. Her eyes had the gleam of naked lust. He could see the outline of her waist, lovely legs, feet small, toenails painted. One ankle wore a thin gold chain with a gold heart affixed.

Logs crackled in the fireplace. Stone knew the time had come for him to jump on top of her or get the hell out. He reached for the bottle of champagne and refilled their glasses. Part of him wanted to rip her gown off, another said *don't you dare.*

He loved Marie, but Belle McGuinness was a short reach away. The champagne made him light-headed. Her perfume drew him closer. *I've got to control myself, because I'm engaged to somebody else.* His hand shook as he sipped the champagne.

She wondered what was wrong with him. This had never

happened to her before. Surely he knew why he was here. "Are you sick?"

"Champagne's going to my head," he alibied.

She lay practically naked beside him. But Marie was in the room. Duty and lust ripped him apart.

"What's wrong?" she asked. Her diamond earrings danced as she refilled their glasses. "Don't you like girls?"

Her nipple touched his arm. The fragrance of her body made him dizzy. He swallowed hard. The artery in his neck pumped harder. The blond beast inside him awakened.

"I'm in love with another woman. I'm supposed to marry her. I can't . . . I just can't."

He felt exhausted. His whole life was a fight. Nothing ever came out right. He leaned against the sofa and closed his eyes.

"I envy her," Belle said wistfully. "Wish somebody loved me like that. But you ain't seen her for how long? Momma's here right now." She pressed her lips against his ear. "I won't hurt you. What're you savin' yourself for? For all you know, she's doing the same thing. Pretty women don't stay alone long. Take it from one who knows."

Stone stared at Belle's bosom spilling out of her nightgown. The champagne made him feel floaty. His eyes roved over her body. *I don't have to tell Marie when I find her. A slice from a cut loaf will never be missed.*

He emptied his glass, set it on the table, and buried his face in his hands. Torn between loyalty to Marie and desire for the naked woman beside him, he muttered, "I don't know what to do."

She pressed against him, inserted the tip of her tongue into his ear. He melted like ice in the tropics. She pushed him onto his back and crawled on top of him. His arms wrapped around her as if they had a life of their own. She squirmed against him and pressed her lips to his. Their tongues touched, electricity shot through him.

He lifted the hem of her gown. She covered his face with impassioned kisses. They tore each other's clothes. The fire cast weird shadows on their entwined bodies as they sank deeper into the cushions.

4

STONE AWOKE IN Belle McGuinness's bed during the middle
of the night. She cuddled against him in sleep, pitch-blackness,
silent, the fragrance of her perfume permeated the air.

He never experienced anything like her. She knew tricks
he never dreamed of. A cold dagger pierced his heart. *What
will Marie and I say to each other when we meet? I'm sorry?
Sorry for what? Is Marie just a silly dream? Why can't I
forget her?*

Even now, lying in bed with Belle, he missed Marie. She'd
touched him deeper than anyone else. He felt as though they
were one person. It never happened before with any other
woman, even Belle with her repertoire of fabulous whorehouse tricks.

The walls closed in on him. He lifted Belle's arm and rolled
out of bed, gathered his clothes, put them on. He stepped into
the corridor and descended the stairs.

A sleepy whore and her drunken miner staggered down
the corridor, the wall splotched where a bottle of whiskey struck it. Only two bartenders were on duty in the
saloon. A croupier spun the chuck-a-luck wheel, hoping
to squeeze every penny from his only customer, a little
old miner wearing knickers and a hat with a high-peaked
crown.

Stone walked out the front door and stood on the veranda.
The moon sat on the far horizon. A few miners shuffled along

the sidewalks, several slept on benches in front of stores closed for the night.

Stone walked to the first alley, heading for the open country. Drunks slept against walls, curled up like children, empty bottles nearby. He came to the next street, a few small saloons spilling forlorn light onto the sidewalks. Stone felt like a ghost as he made his way through the next alley. Couldn't be faithful to Marie. He shook his head bitterly. *Now what do I have?*

He thought of Belle, hardly knew who she was. What could come of it? He was just her passing fancy. Tomorrow she'd find somebody else, a woman like that loyal only to herself.

He needed somebody he could rely on. Marie and he'd been through too much together, his interlude with Belle just one of those things.

"John Stone," said a voice in a doorway.

Stone yanked both Colts. A shadow moved, Tommy Moran appeared, holding both his empty hands in the air.

"I wanted to talk with you, John Stone."

Stone kept both Colts aimed, wondered if somebody was behind him. He glanced backward quickly.

"I'm alone," Moran said. "This ain't no bushwhack. I wanted to kill you, would've done it in the Grand Palace. That's what I come to tell you about. I din't want you to think I'm afraid of you." He removed his hat. "We met once before, long time ago."

Stone narrowed his eyes and examined Moran in the light of the moon. "Don't remember you."

"Antietam, the second day, in the afternoon. That ring a bell? I fought for the Union, you were a rebel cavalry officer, damn near killed me. But then you stopped and let me live. Remember?"

"Maybe it was somebody looked like me."

"Never forget your face. You saved my life." Moran glanced furtively behind him. "Somebody paid me to kill you. He'd shoot me if he found out I told you, but I'm pullin' stakes tonight. It was Maaa . . ."

A shot rang out, Moran shuddered, Stone dropped to the ground, both Colts ready to fire. The assassin's gun flashed again at the back entrance to the alley. Stone cut loose a four-shot barrage that sounded like thunder. Moran lay beside him, clutching his stomach. Lights came on in buildings nearby.

"What the hell's goin' on out there!"

Stone rolled Moran onto his back. Moran gasped as he tried to speak. "Kkkkkkk . . ."

Moran went still. His eyes glazed over and jaw dropped open. Stone wasn't a doctor, but saw dead men before. A deputy blew a whistle. Stone ducked into a doorway and listened to the tumult in the street. They'd remember his quarrel with Moran earlier in the saloon. Men had been hung for less. He had to get back to the Grand Palace without being seen.

Kincaid latched the door behind him, leaned against the wall, and took a deep breath. His heart beat like a drum. His whole operation nearly blew up in his face, but he saved it with two lucky shots. *Can't trust nobody,* he thought ruefully.

He had caught a scrap of the conversation between Stone and Moran. *That's what happens when you look for a bargain.* He climbed the stairs to his bedroom.

"Where were you?" his wife asked sleepily.

"I ain't left yer side all night."

"Come to bed."

Kincaid took off his clothes and crawled under the covers. Her arm fell across his chest. He stared at the ceiling. *First thing in the morning, hire the fastest available gun to kill John Stone.*

Belle McGuinness looked through the peephole. It was John Stone. "Where've you been?"

"Somebody got shot." Agitated, he paced back and forth on the rug and told the story. "Thought they'd arrest me, so I ran away. Probably looking for me right now."

"Tell 'em you spent the night here. I'll back yer story."

"You don't have to drag your reputation through the mud for me. I'll fend for myself."

"My reputation can't be worse than it is already, and I don't give a damn anyway. If the marshal bothers you, send him to me. I can handle that son of a bitch. Come on to bed."

"Does anyone know who Kincaid was before he came here?"

"I told you: In Lodestone, we don't ask people where they come from."

"He just showed up one day?"

"That's what all of us did, includin' you. Why're you askin' so many questions about Kincaid?"

"He makes me curious."

She kissed his throat. "You make me horny."

The second time is always easier. She led him to the bed, peeled away his clothes. He didn't have strength to resist. She tossed her nightgown over her head, revealing a figure that reminded him of a Rubens painting. Stone closed his eyes. She lowered herself onto him. He felt electrified. *I'll worry about this some other time.*

A short distance away, Rebecca Hawkins prayed in the cellar of her home. Naked, a bloody cat-o'-nine-tails gripped tightly in her hand, her back and buttocks striated with welts, she bowed her head in the darkness.

"Purify me, O Lord. Cast out my wickedness and sin. Make me worthy of you."

She raised the whip and lashed her back, the pain exquisitely delicious. The whore of Babylon and John Stone could be vanquished with a mere glance if her faith were strong. She danced on the cold hard-packed earth, punishing herself for the memory of John Stone's arms. "Out, Beelzebub! Away with you, Satan."

The whip whistled through the air and came down on her scarred and bloody back. She shivered with pain and delight. "Make me victorious over thine enemies."

The whip wrapped round her body, digging into her flesh. Exaltation came over her. She dropped to her knees, sobbing and sniffling. Her body trembled uncontrollably, floor covered with dots of blood. Darkness spun around her, she fell, banging her cheek on the way down. She whimpered and went slack. A black pool drew her toward its vortex. Waves of ecstasy passed over her.

5

THE CORPSE OF Tommy Moran lay face down on the table, skin turning pale blue. Dr. White removed a lump of lead from a hole cut into his back. "Looks like a forty-four."

Marshal Kincaid screwed up his eyes as he examined it. Forty-four all right, from his own gun.

"Shot him twice in the back," Dr. White said. "Didn't even give him a chance. What kind of man'd shoot another in the back?"

Kincaid said nothing. Any man would shoot another in the back, if he had to.

"Any idea who did it?" Dr. White asked.

"The new bartender at the Grand Palace, name of John Stone. He and Moran got into it last night. They was a-ready to draw on each other."

"You figger Stone bushwhacked him?"

"He don't have a good alibi, he'll spend the night in the cooler. He puts up a fuss, you'll be a-seein' 'im right here in this room a-fore sundown."

The atmosphere was icy at the Madden breakfast table. Gail buttered her corn muffin and wished she hadn't come to Lodestone. Unwittingly, she'd dropped into the middle of a bad marriage.

The walls in the house were thin. She heard her sister and brother-in-law arguing most of the night. Patricia accused Bart

52

of keeping another woman, he denied it vehemently. They'd gone round and round. Gail wanted to get out of the house. She ate quickly, gulped down her coffee, said, "I'd like to take a little walk."

Her sister raised her eyebrows. "Are you crazy? Don't you know what's out there?"

"I was looking out the window before, it didn't seem *that* bad."

"This city," her sister replied, "is full of inebriated miners armed to the teeth, and there's a woman shortage. No telling what they might do to a pretty young thing like you."

"Don't scare her needlessly," Bart said, flashing his smile. "They'd never bother anybody who looked like a lady. It's the poor soiled doves who get the abuse, but they can usually handle themselves."

"Who'd know better than you?" Patricia asked, caustic innuendo in her voice. She turned to her sister. "The most notorious prostitute in Lodestone is a woman named Belle McGuinness. She's slept with everybody important and unimportant, and now's the richest woman in town. She parades around like a lady, and many of this town's foremost gentlemen are in love with her. I guess there's no accounting for some people's taste." She shot her husband an angry glance.

He maintained his smile. No matter what he felt inside, he could turn it on.

"I can go alone," Gail said. "I walked in Boston by myself, nothing happened to me."

"The good citizens of Boston don't wear guns," Patricia said. "The point I'm trying to make is the men here are heavily armed, and never hesitate to shoot."

"She's right." Bart pulled a derringer from an inner pocket of his frock coat. "Even I carry one. You never know when you might need it."

"Have you ever used it?" Gail asked.

"Not yet." He handed it to her. "Take it with you. Might come in handy. You never know. I have more upstairs."

Patricia reached across the table and grabbed the derringer. "She's liable to shoot herself with it! How can you give an inexperienced person a loaded gun? Are you crazy?"

"Protection," Bart said. "Every woman in the West should know how to use one." He turned to Gail. "I'd be happy to give you shooting lessons."

"You'll give her no such thing!" Patricia said. "You keep away from her!"

"Only trying to be helpful to my sister-in-law, dear."

Gail pushed back her chair. "I don't need a gun. I'll stay on the main streets, and it's broad daylight. I doubt anything will happen."

She climbed the stairs to her room. Bart and Patricia sat facing each other across the dining-room table. Slowly and deliberately, Patricia raised the derringer and pointed it at her husband's chest. He continued to smile, though beads of perspiration appeared on his forehead.

"You ever lay one of your filthy hands on my sister, I'll kill you," she said evenly.

"This has nothing to do with your sister, and you know it. You're jealous of Belle McGuinness, but I swear to you, you're wrong."

"I'm not wrong. I know what you're up to. You're disgracing me."

Patricia sighted down the barrel. Bart's smile faltered. They heard footsteps on the stairs. Gail's feet came into view. Bart snatched the derringer out of his wife's hands.

Gail wore a plaid wool coat and bonnet, carried a purse. She waved to her sister and brother-in-law as she made her way to the door.

"Don't go too far," Patricia warned. "Keep your wits about you. Expect you back for lunch at twelve-thirty. Don't talk to strange men, and whatever you do, don't get too close to saloons. Worst of them all is the Grand Palace. When you see it, cross over to the other side of the street. And watch out for stray bullets. Do you hear?"

Cool breeze blew through the open window of Belle's boudoir. She opened her eyes to the new day. Her arms wrapped around John Stone, she felt full of hope and joy.

Usually she awoke cranky, her days spent scheming and plotting cynically. But not today. Today would be different. She nudged him. "Wake up."

"Want to sleep," he mumbled.

"No time. Got to teach you the saloon business. Anything I can't stand, it's a lazy man. What you like for breakfast?"

"Lots."

"When I come back, I'll 'spect you to be ready to eat."

She tied on her robe and left the boudoir. Stone rolled onto his back, put on his pants near the window, the street full of wagons, carriages, individuals on horseback, stamp mill pounded in the distance. He opened the window a crack, noxious odor entered the room. He poured water into the basin, washed hands and face. Belle returned. "Breakfast'll be ready in ten minutes. You'll need new clothes, by the way. The manager of the Grand Palace Saloon wears a suit."

"I don't have money for clothes."

"Go to the haberdashery across the street. Put them on my account. The Grand Palace ain't no bust-out joint."

Stone frowned. *Beware of any enterprise that requires new clothes,* said Henry David Thoreau. "Why do I have to wear a suit?"

"Goes with the territory."

"Find yourself another manager."

He headed toward the closet. Her face mottled with emotion. He took his fringed buckskin coat off the hanger.

"You win," she said. "Wear what you want."

Defeat was in her voice. Stone didn't like the sound of it. Just to get his way over a matter of no real consequence. He wrapped his arms around her. "I'll get a suit," he said, "but I'm keeping my old Confederate cavalry hat and my guns."

She liquefied in his arms. *He gave in to me. Maybe he really loves me.* She raised on her tiptoes and kissed his lips.

The maid entered. "Marshal Kincaid here to see you, ma'am. Says it's important."

"Send him in."

Belle separated herself from Stone. "I'll do the talking." She looked into the mirror and applied cosmetics. Stone adjusted his guns. Kincaid entered the boudoir, hat in hand, badge shining on his brown leather vest. His eyes fell on Stone.

"Just the man I'm lookin' fer," Kincaid said. "You're under arrest for the murder of Tommy Moran."

"I been here in this room all night," Stone replied.

"That's right," Belle added. "We was in that bed, and I wouldn't let him get away."

Kincaid's brow furrowed. Belle ordinarily wasn't so brazen about her affairs. "What time you two go to bed?"

"Two in the mornin'. Stayed there until a half hour ago, ain't that right, honey?"

"Sure is," Stone replied.

"That all, Marshal?" Belle asked. "Let me introduce you to my new manager."

Kincaid smiled thinly at Stone. "Comin' up fast in this town, ain't you?"

"Only stayin' a month, Marshal. Got business in San Francisco."

"Yer boss might have somethin' to say about that. She is yer boss, ain't she? She says jump, and you do it like a trained dog, am I right?"

Stone stood erectly in front of the dresser, shoulders squared. "That badge doesn't mean a goddamn thing to me."

"Want me to take it off?"

"Up to you."

"Watch yer step. You might get hit by a stray bullet someday, like Tommy Moran."

"Where were *you* last night when Tommy Moran was shot?"

"I ask the questions, not you."

"I'm the new city reporter for the *Lodestone Gazette*. Where were you when Tommy Moran got bushwhacked?"

"Kiss my ass." Kincaid walked out the door. Belle waited until his footsteps could no longer be heard. "Why'd you rile him?" she asked Stone. "I tried to smooth everythin' over, but you made it worse. Kincaid is dangerous. They say he used to be a gunfighter."

"Who said that?"

"Feller passed through town once, said he knew him when."

"Bet the feller didn't hang around long."

"Matter of fact he didn't. But don't mess with Kincaid. It ain't healthy."

"You stood up to him pretty well."

"Nobody pushes Belle McGuinness around."

"They don't push around John Stone either."

Her features softened. "That's why we're together. We're the same kind of people." She embraced him. "Oh, Johnny, I'm so glad I found you!"

• • •

The maid, Maxine Goines, escorted Marshal Kincaid to the door. She reached for the knob, he placed his hand on her wrist. "Somethin' I want you to do fer me," he said in a low voice.

Maxine was afraid of him. "What you want, Marshal? I'm awful busy right now."

He reached into his pocket and pulled out a twenty-dollar gold eagle. "I wanna know what Belle and her new beau talk about. You'll get one of these every week, but you ever lie to me, I'll kill you."

"I don't want no trouble, Mr. Marshal. Don't gimme no money. I don't hear nothin' and I don't know nothin'. I'm just the maid."

He took her hand and forced the coin into it. "You'd better start findin' out things, you want to go on livin'."

Semiclad whores left their doors open and hollered to each other across the hallways as they bathed. Slipchuck followed his broom from room to room.

"Hey there—you got a match?" a blonde asked.

"Why shore." Slipchuck scratched a match on the seat of his pants. The whore held her cigarette in dainty fingers and puffed blue smoke.

"Do folks what work here git a special rate?" he asked.

"Special rate fer what?" she replied, glancing askance at him.

"You know what." He winked. "A little lovin'."

"You git yer pay, come see Sally. I'll take good care of you."

Slipchuck returned to the corridor and resumed sweeping. Kincaid strode toward him, puffing his corncob pipe. "Mornin', Marshal. Gittin' a li'l poontang are ye?"

"Not today," Kincaid replied, descending the next flight of stairs.

A young whore wrapped in a towel approached from the far end of the corridor. She had long slim legs, the kind a man liked wrapped around his neck. *Thank God she can't see what I'm thinkin'.*

She slapped him on the ass as she passed by. "Put yer eyes back in yer head, you old fart. Ain't you never see'd girls a-fore?"

• • •

Stone crossed the floor of the Grand Palace Saloon. One roulette wheel, one chuck-a-luck, a few card games, not much doing. Drunks left over from last night snoring on tables while newcomers drank their first whiskey of the day. Stone checked liquor stocks, carried a few crates and kegs in from the still.

On his last trip, something at a corner table caught his eye. A young miner pulled out his gun. Stone set down the keg of beer, yanked his Colts. The miner turned the barrel around and pointed it to his head.

Stone ran toward him, dived, grabbed his wrist. The miner didn't put up a struggle. He bowed his head and wept. Stone sat opposite him and examined his face, mid-twenties, short black beard, sorrow and fatigue in his eyes. "Want to talk about it?" Stone asked soothingly.

The miner shrugged. "Nothin' to talk about. Went bust, what else?"

"You're young, you can start out all over again. I happen to have a bartendering position open right here. When can you start?"

"It ain't just me. I lost my paw's money in the mine, an' my girlfriend's paw put in a bundle too. We're all ruined. There ain't no gold in that ground. Maybe was once, but not now."

"I read about a strike in the *Lodestone Gazette*."

"All that rag prints is lies. I don't know what I'm going to do. You should've let me kill myself while I was in the mood."

"Won't solve anything. I think you should accept my job offer. You've still got plenty of time to make something of yourself."

"We all think we'll hit the mother lode if we dig down through the next ledge. But all we ever do is dig, and throw money into that goddamn stinking hole in the ground."

A Franciscan monk in a brown gown carried a big burlap bag marked BEANS to a wagon. A gentleman dressed like a Boston lawyer strolled along the sidewalk as if on Beacon Hill. A horse urinated into the gutter. Gail wrinkled her nose at the strong odor. The stamp mill slammed ore into powder on a hill in the distance.

The sidewalk was crowded, men armed to the teeth, but no one bothered her. They had the same swagger as lumberjacks in Maine. Men who weren't afraid to fight. A whole town full of them. A few other women could be seen, modestly dressed. At the corner: GRAND PALACE.

She gazed at the imposing structure, biggest she'd seen in town so far. The second floor had a balcony, a few prostitutes sunning themselves. Gail wondered what their lives were like. They didn't appear unhappy. Gail shuddered at the thought of giving herself to a man she didn't love.

Music radiated through the walls and windows of the building. She heard a man shout for joy. A den of iniquity, no doubt about it. *Maybe I can get a closer look.* She wondered how to cross the muddy street. The other women lifted their skirts and plowed through.

She paused at the edge of the sidewalk and looked ahead apprehensively. A horse's leg went in the muck halfway to his knee. *I'll never make it.*

"Hello there, little lady. Wanna git across the street?"

She shielded her face with her hand and looked at a tall bearded miner wearing a floppy brimmed hat with a high round crown. "Mud's too deep," she said. "Think I'd better try at the corner."

"Hell, I'll take you acrost!"

Before she could open her mouth, he swept her off her feet. The only place to put her arms were around his neck. He plodded resolutely into the middle of the street. Gail felt violated in some way. She didn't even know him! A gigantic ox turd lay half submerged in the muck. If she insisted he let her down, she'd sink up to her neck.

They reached the far side of the street. He set her down. "You ever need somebody to carry you agin', jest holler for Kevin McGeachy, hear?"

He tipped his hat and walked away.

She turned to the Grand Palace. The music was a reel. Men laughed heartily within the planked walls. The windows were covered with drapes. *What goes on there?*

Frightened and curious, Gail wanted to peep through the window, but a drunken miner might shoot her. She tried to imagine what it looked like, based on illustrations of western saloons she'd seen in magazines.

One of the Grand Palace doors opened. John Stone headed toward her, pulling the brim of his hat low over his eyes. She waved to him. "I was wondering what happened to you. Where'd you sleep last night?"

Stone pointed his thumb backward to the Grand Palace. He spent the night in a whorehouse? She didn't know what to say.

"What're you doing here?" he asked.

"Just taking a walk. How about you?"

"Got a job at the Grand Palace. Managing the saloon."

"That was fast."

"Sometimes it happens that way. Also working for the local newspaper. If you ever see a shooting, let me know. The editor is big on shootings."

"Sounds like you've had a busy night."

"Hope things settle down today. A man can only handle so much change."

She glanced behind him at the Grand Palace. "What's it like in there?"

"Big barn."

"Gambling?"

"That's the main reason for the place. Want to take a quick look?"

He caught her hand and led her toward the door. She dug in her heels, but he was too strong. A miner with a walrus mustache and buck teeth held the door, she swept into the murky depths of the Grand Palace Saloon.

First thing she saw was a chuck-a-luck wheel spinning and clacking. Miners watched the wheel avidly, chips piled high on the table. Other miners stood at long bars on three walls of the establishment. More miners gambled at tables, air stank of whiskey and tobacco smoke, floor filthy. A whore sat on a miner's lap, his hand somewhere up her dress.

"Think I've had enough."

"You just got here. The whole second floor's a whorehouse."

"Not today." She headed toward the door.

"More people at night," he said apologetically, "they have a stage show."

Outside, she took a deep draught of fresh air. "Unhealthiest place I've ever been in."

"Nothing else to do in a town like this except go to the saloon." He saw the clock beside the Lodestone Savings Bank. "Got an appointment. Nice seeing you again."

He strolled away, a frown on his face. Marie was in San Francisco, Belle in the Grand Palace, now he felt strong romantic feelings for Gail Petigru. A man's an alley cat unless he controls his appetites.

Stone had a headache due to insufficient sleep and the champagne he'd drunk the previous night. He tried not to think about Marie, but she shimmered before him on the sidewalk, looking at him reproachfully. "I couldn't help it," he muttered. "I never claimed to be a saint."

Angry at himself and the world, he made his way to the offices of the *Lodestone Gazette*. Impossible for a man to lead a decent life. Too many temptations. Haven't seen Marie for seven years. *What do you expect of me?*

Your loyalty forever, Marie replied.

He remembered what Kevin McGeachy told him. All women nag. Even when they're five hundred miles away. He wished he could escape Marie, but yearned for her. She could nag all she wanted, if they were together. His mind full of Marie, he'd forgotten the woman he'd just slept with.

Belle soaked in the bathtub, humming a tune. She felt lighthearted and young, bubbles bursting in the water around her. He had everything she wanted.

Won't be easy to keep him, he's younger than me, can't tie a man like that down. But he feels something. A man can't fake what he did. In all her days, never ran into anybody like him. She raised the mirror and looked at four red marks on her shoulder, left by his teeth. Was he like this with all women?

It began slow, but he stoked her fires until she was insane. The water was getting cool. "Maxine?" *The only time I really need her is when I take a bath. Where the hell is she?*

Belle climbed out of the bathtub, put on her robe. Dripping water to the floor, she made her way to the kitchen. No hot water on the stove, fire in the box dying down. "Maxine!" Belle worried that something had happened to her. She wandered through the top floor of the Grand Palace, calling her name.

Maxine had disappeared.

• • •

Bart Madden sat in his office, stock certificates piled around him, in the safe, in drawers. Most of what he owned was mining stock and real estate. *This region needs another major strike. Then I'll sell everything and get the hell out of here.*

His clerk opened the door. "Marshal Kincaid to see you, sir."

Madden wondered if it was time to give the marshal another payoff. The marshal's wide shoulders filled the doorway, hadn't bothered to take his hat off, a bad sign. The door closed behind him. Marshal Kincaid sauntered toward the desk and grinned. "Drifter name of John Stone spent the night with Belle McGuinness, accordin' to testimony she just gave me."

A needle of jealousy pierced Madden's heart. He tried to find his voice, but Kincaid spoke first.

"I seen Stone with my own eyes in her bedroom. They was both half-undressed. Looked like they'd been a-goin' at it all night. Never seen Belle a-lookin' so satisfied."

Madden kept himself under control with great difficulty. "I'm sure you didn't come here just to retell cheap gossip, Marshal. What's on your mind?"

Kincaid sat on the edge of the desk. "I know everything that goes on in this town. Belle was your woman, ain't that right?"

"What's it to you?"

"How'd you like to get rid of John Stone?"

"What do you mean, *get rid of him?*"

"You know what I'm talking about. Kill the son of a bitch. What say we hire somebody to shoot him down?"

Madden leaned back and folded his hands on his belly. "Got anybody in mind?"

"There's a few good fellers in town, but John Stone is a fast hand. Heard he shot Tod Buckalew, one of the best in Kansas. We can't send a local boy agin' somebody like that. I heard Randy LaFollette's in Denver. We could hire him for five hundred dollars."

"Do we need the best? Can't you find a few local guns to bushwhack him for less than that?"

"If he shot Tod Buckalew, he's better'n anybody in this town. Don't it bother you that he stole yer woman right out from underneath yer nose?"

Madden narrowed his eyes. "Why do *you* want him dead, Marshal? What's he done to you?"

"None of yer goddamned business."

"Must be quite interesting, I'd wager."

"Don't put yer nose where it don't belong, Mr. Banker Man. Do we hire Randy LaFollette, or don't we?"

"Can't you get him cheaper?"

"You don't bargain with The Undertaker. Pay his price or let John Stone keep a-screwin' Belle McGuinness."

Madden's head felt as if somebody pounded it with a hammer. "I'll go half with you," he replied in a strangled voice. "Send Randy LaFollette a telegram."

John Stone saw the sign: LODESTONE GAZETTE. It was mounted atop a boxy one-story building next to a forge, the blacksmith's hammer beating contrapuntally to the pounding of the stamp mill. A group of men on horseback road by, splattering the cuffs of Stone's pants with mud. Stone thought the big town disgusting, couldn't wait to leave.

He crossed the street carefully, nearly losing his right boot in the muck. A rat scurried across the alley between the *Gazette* building and the shack on the other side, which sported a sign: GOLDEN NUGGET SALOON.

Stone opened the door of the *Lodestone Gazette*. Edgar Faraday sat at the front desk, writing furiously on a notepad. In back, a man wearing a green visor worked a big four-legged press, smell of ink in the air. "Where's your story, young man? Should've been on my desk two hours ago. Where the hell you been?"

Stone pushed his hat to the back of his head. "Got a new job."

"Thought we had a deal."

"Belle McGuinness offered me a hundred dollars a month to manage the Grand Palace."

Faraday arose from his chair. "Journalism is a noble profession," he said dramatically. "A newspaper is the conscience of a community. Would you rather sell whiskey and beer to drunken miners, or transform the course of history?"

"I'm trying to get to San Francisco as soon as possible. But a saloon might be the ideal spot for a newspaper reporter. Maybe

I could handle both jobs. By the way, I was with Tommy Moran when he was shot last night. He said he was hired to gun me down."

"Why should anybody want you killed?"

"Damned if I know."

"Sit at the desk over there and write the story."

"Got to get back to the Grand Palace. Been years since I wrote anything."

"Just give me the facts. I'll rewrite it. Circulation always goes up after a good shooting."

"Is it true the mines're tapped out?"

"Who told you that?"

"Somebody in the saloon."

"Lots of rumors in a boom town. We only print the truth."

"Might be something to follow up."

Faraday looked exasperated. "I told you before, we don't want depressing news. Folks are interested in dramatic incidents, like people getting shot and such."

"If you found out the gold is gone, sell a lot of newspapers."

"Sure, for a few weeks. Then there won't be any town left. Getting too old for poverty, my boy. Give the people what they want. That's what I say."

"You think they don't want to know the mines're tapped out?"

"How do you know they're tapped out? Might be ten tons of solid gold beneath this very building. Sit down and write your story." Faraday flipped a ten-dollar coin at Stone. "Here's another advance on your salary. We got a newpaper to publish."

Marshal Kincaid entered the train station. Travelers with luggage sat on benches, waiting for the afternoon train to Denver. Nailed to the wall was a print of a locomotive puffing steam. A man with a white mustache sat in a cage, reading a timetable.

Marshal Kincaid opened the door beside the cage. Bags of mail and crates were stacked on the floor of the back room, a man weighed a parcel on a scale. Against the right wall, an operator slept beside the telegraph key. Marshal Kincaid shook his shoulder.

"Got a message to send," Kincaid said, dropping a sheet of paper on the desk.

The telegrapher read the scrawled words.

To: Randy LaFollette, Crown Hotel, Denver
Assignment in Lodestone. Standard rate.
Begin immediately.
Marshal Kincaid

"Don't tell anybody about this telegram," Kincaid said. "If you know what's good for you."

Belle stepped onto the veranda of the Grand Palace, the bright mountain sunlight seared her eyes. She seldom left the building, but today had something to do.

She was the most notorious, richest woman in town. Her clothing followed the style of New York, she was bedecked with jewels, wore no cosmetics, face pale as fine Italian marble, lips thinner and more subtly curved. She might be a young mother, the wife of a prominent citizen, actress at the Lodestone Opera House, instead of an ex-prostitute.

Accompanied by Boggs, her bodyguard, no one dared say a word. He wore a derby hat with suit and vest, but needed a shave, his hair unruly, brown eyes suspicious. Belle picked up her dress as she maneuvered over boards thrown on the mud in the street. On the other side, she saw a sign: GUNS.

Behind the counter, a man with white chin whiskers folded his copy of the *Lodestone Gazette*. "Howdy, Miss McGuinness," said Homer Tomlinson nervously, because he'd been one of her customers in the old days. "What can I do fer you?"

"Like to buy a derringer."

"What price range?"

"Don't matter."

He pulled a tray of derringers out of the display case. The tiny lethal weapons lay on purple velvet. Her eyes fell on a gold-plated Remington over-and-under with mother-of-pearl grips. She picked it up and held it in her dainty hand.

"Good choice," he said. "Gives you that extra shot. Comes with a leather pouch on a thong." He held it up. "Don't need

a pocket or a purse. Just hang it 'round yer neck. Want some
ammunition?"

"One box."

He told her the price. She nodded to Boggs. He reached
into his pocket and pulled out coins.

"I'd like to have the barrel engraved," Belle said.

"Take care of it for you," said Tomlinson. He passed her
paper and a pen.

She wrote:

> to Johnny
> with love always
> from Belle

Rebecca Hawkins knelt before a bare cross in her living
room, praying since dawn. She was the daughter of a preacher who'd gone mad and had to be put away, her mother a
well-known religious fanatic who convinced her to fight the
devil constantly. You shall know him by his fruit.

She clasped her hands tightly in prayer, her knees hurt, trying
to starve the pleasurable memory of her butt resting in John
Stone's arms. A knock on the door. For a moment, Rebecca
didn't know where she was. Her devotions transported her to
far-off places. She opened the front door.

Mrs. Marples pointed her umbrella toward the center of
town. "The whore is flaunting herself in broad daylight! Miss
Hawkins, we can't let her get away with it!"

John Stone saw the sign: ASSAYER'S OFFICE. It hung over a
door on the second floor. He climbed the stairs on the outside
of the building and looked over the town. Buildings extended
into the foothills of nearby mountains denuded of trees for the
stamp mill. An eagle flew across the sky. What did it think of
the huge metropolis in the mountains? Beside the door was a
nameplate:

> Jonas Brodbent
> Assayer and Engineer

A short bald man with black sideburns sat at a rolltop desk.
"What can I do for you?"

"I'm John Stone, reporter for the *Lodestone Gazette*. Wanted to ask you a few questions."

Brodbent smiled, showing monkey teeth. "Always glad to help your fine publication. Don't believe I've seen you before. New in town?"

"Heard rumors the mines're tapped out in this area. When's the last time a good new strike was reported?"

"Happens all the time."

"Name me a mine that struck gold in the last month."

"Can't think of any off the top of my head. They change so often. Buy and sell each other."

"Do you remember the name of a person who struck it rich?"

Brodbent held out his hands. "I don't keep track of stuff like that. All I do is test samples."

"You know what I think? This town's gone bust, but doesn't know it yet."

Brodbent leaned forward in his chair. "You print that lie, you're in trouble. That's friendly advice. I'd take it, I were you."

"You're not me."

Stone descended the stairs. A wagon full of crates rolled by, pulled by a team of oxen. The bullwhacker cracked his whip. "Git on, you sons of bitches!"

Stone's worst suspicions were confirmed by Brodbent's reaction to his comments. If an assayer can't furnish evidence of gold ore, maybe there isn't any. Next stop City Hall, where records of mines are kept.

"There it is, ma'am," said Tomlinson, handing the derringer to Belle.

She read the engraving. "You did a good job."

"I hope the gentleman appreciates the kindness of your gesture."

"He don't, I'll shoot his ass."

He wrapped the derringer in brown paper and handed it to Boggs, who dropped it into his carpetbag. There was a furor behind her in the street.

"What's goin' on out there!" She walked to the window and looked outside. The street was full of women in black dresses, led by Rebecca Hawkins. They formed a barricade between her and the Grand Palace.

"There she is!" hollered the preacher lady, pointing to the pale face in the window of the store. "The whore of Babylon!"

Frightened, Belle took a step backward, a scream of victory arose from the throats of the women. But Belle's moment of shame passed. "They're a-screwin' with the wrong woman." She turned to Tomlinson. "You got a double-barreled shotgun?"

"Don't want no trouble!" he protested, holding up his hands.

"Sell me a shotgun, or my man here'll beat the livin' shit out of you!"

Tomlinson looked at Jamie Boggs, muscles bursting the seams of his suit. In the street, the woman chanted: "Whore—whore—whore!"

Belle banged her fist on the counter. Her rage came on like a hurricane. "Where's that shotgun! I ain't got all day!"

Tomlinson also hated the religious women. He reached toward the wall and took down a double-barreled shotgun. "Already loaded. You'll blow a hole right through the middle of 'em."

Belle wheeled and faced the door. "I'll lead the way, Jamie. If they try to stop me, pick up the pieces."

Jamie motioned frantically, making gurgling sounds.

"I know you want to go first," she replied, "but this is my fight. I don't hide behind men when I'm a-fightin' women!"

She yanked open the door angrily and leveled the shotgun at the mob of religious ladies arrayed before her.

"There she is!" Rebecca yelled. "The devil's bride herself! We've got her cornered!"

Every man in the vicinity ran for his life at the sight of a woman with a shotgun. Rebecca and her assembly stood defiantly, fists self-righteously down their sides.

Belle walked across the planked sidewalk. The women gathered shoulder to shoulder, black skirts hanging in mud. Belle became angrier with every passing second. Straightlaced bitches. A good solid screw'd kill any one of them. Belle descended the stairs. Her boots sank in the mud to her ankles.

The women surged forward, led by Rebecca. Belle leveled the shotgun at her. "You try to stop me," Belle cried, eyes flashing lightning bolts, "I'll blow you to hell!"

Rebecca pointed her long bony finger at her. "Who knows hell better than the whore of Babylon! Listen to her—hell spills out her filthy mouth! You heard her with your own ears! She's the devil's daughter! Don't let her get away!"

"I'm a-crossin' this road!" Belle retorted. "Anybody tries to stop me, I'll shoot!" Belle's face was deadly as she took her first step. At her side, Jamie tried to form words.

"Go ahead and kill me!" Rebecca screamed. "I'll fly to heaven on the wings of doves!"

Rebecca stormed toward Belle, a collision inevitable. Belle raised the barrel of the shotgun and tightened her finger around the trigger. Rebecca's eyes closed in bliss, a faint smile wreathed her stark features. *The bitch thinks she's going to heaven,* Belle thought. *She's crazy!* Belle eased off the trigger.

Mrs. Shaughnessy screeched. "She's afraid of God's children! She's a-runnin' from us!"

Belle dug her left foot into the ground behind her, aimed at Rebecca again. "I don't run from nobody. If you're crazy enough to come at me, I'm crazy enough to blow yer goddamned fool head off."

Rebecca's eyes blurred. The shotgun in Belle's hand became the infant Jesus. "Behold the handmaiden of God," Rebecca whispered.

"One more step," Belle warned, "you're a dead woman."

Rebecca couldn't hear through choirs of angels singing in her head. She reached for the babe, Belle tightened her finger on the trigger.

Something crashed into her. The shotgun fired like twin cannons. Windows rattled in the Grand Palace. Belle sat in the mud, looking up at Marshal Kincaid.

"What the hell's goin' on!"

Belle got in the first word. "Them bitches're tryin' to keep me out of my establishment!"

"Whorehouse, you mean!" Rebecca replied, back to her senses. "If there was law in this town, this woman be hanged!"

Kincaid turned to her. "Belle's got a right to walk where she wants. You keep it up, I'll put *you* in jail. I'm a-gonna tell you one last time. Clear yer women out of the street, or you'll be arrested."

"You wouldn't dare!"

Kincaid motioned to his deputies. "She's under arrest!"

Two men in blue grabbed her arms, she struggled to break loose. The women swarmed over the deputies. One scratched four sharp fingernails across Kincaid's face. Another kicked his shins. He fell to the mud. A terrific melee erupted in the middle of the street, stopping traffic.

Jamie scooped Belle up in his arms and ran toward the front veranda of the Grand Palace. On the second-floor balcony, whores cheered him on. Slipchuck jumped up and down excitedly, waving both fists in the air.

Two black-garbed women tried to block their path. "Don't let the whore of Babylon get away!"

"Keep goin'!" Belle hollered to Jamie. "Don't stop now!"

Jamie plowed into them, a woman swung her umbrella at Belle's head. Belle caught the instrument in her left hand, drove a sharp right jab into the woman's face. The woman fell back, as her partner tore at Belle's clothes. Belle gave her a backhand smack in the mouth, sent her reeling. Jamie jumped onto the front veranda of the Grand Palace. A smiling bartender opened the door, Jamie carried his boss into her fortress, dress torn and splattered with mud.

In the street, women beat deputies with umbrellas. Belle placed her hands on her hips and laughed heartily. Her voice carried out the door.

The tumult ended as suddenly as it began. Everyone turned to Belle.

"She who laughs now," hollered Rebecca, "will cry later! Those who are high will be brought low! Like Sodom and Gomorrah, this building will be destroyed!" She looked around. *I've got their attention again. O Lord, make them listen to me.* She felt dizzy, reached to one of her women for support. "Gentlemen—don't go near this place! It's the devil's house! That woman may be beautiful in the flesh, but putrid in the spirit! Turn away from sin! Never drink the devil's brew! Come with me now, let us pray for the destruction of this evil place!"

She bowed her head, imagined everyone praying with her. Together, they'd blow down the walls of Jericho.

"Take more'n a prayer to tear this place down!" Belle replied. "The Grand Palace was built by the smartest carpenters, and we got the oldest whiskey, prettiest girls, best musicians, and most fun west of the Mississippi! Plenty of room fer ev'rybody! Drinks on the house!"

A roar arose from the crowd stampeding like cattle toward the doors. Rebecca opened her eyes. Men elbowed each other in their haste to get inside the hellhole. The preacher lady rose to her feet. Another unanswered prayer. *When will You show Yourself to me?*

6

JONAS BRODBENT ENTERED Madden's office. "The new reporter for the Lodestone Gazette just said the gold's petered out, and he's going to write about it! You'd better talk with Faraday right away!"

"Who's the new reporter?"

"John Stone."

Madden stared into space. "What's he look like?"

"Dangerous. On his way to City Hall to check records."

"He won't find anything there."

"Maybe it's time to salt another mine."

"Been thinking about that myself. You know somebody who'll take care of it?"

"Got just the man. You'd better have a talk with Faraday in the meantime."

"Tell him I want to speak with him, and don't worry about the story. It won't be written."

City Hall, a two-story wooden building in the center of Lodestone, sat opposite a park with benches and a flagpole flying Old Glory. In the land registration office, an elderly man with thick eyeglasses sat behind a desk and scratched a pen on paper. A map of the territory hung on the wall. "What can I do for you?"

"Just hit town," replied Stone. "Wonder if you could show me where gold's been discovered lately. Want to get close to the mother lode as I can."

The old man shrugged. "I knew where the mother lode was, I'd be digging with the rest of them."

"Thought I read in the *Lodestone Gazette* about a gold strike a few days ago."

"Don't believe everything you read in the papers. You want to know about gold, go to the stamp mill. That's where they extract the stuff. The foreman should be able to tell you where the best samples're comin' from, but there's no guarantee you'll find gold there. Might be a million dollars underneath your chair, nothing beneath mine. Used to be a prospector myself, lost my shirt. But don't let me discourage you. Millionaires were made in this territory."

"Name one."

"Jacob Sloat. Lives on the top floor of the Sheffield. Joe Grigsby's up there too. So's Jeff Depew. They're the first to strike it rich in Lodestone."

"No strikes since then?"

"A man could make his boodle and leave without saying anything. You want to find out about gold, ask at the stamp mill. That's where it all ends up sooner or later."

Jonas Brodbent saw John Stone walk out the front door of City Hall. The assayer ducked into an alley, hoping he hadn't been seen. He circled, entered the rear door of City Hall, climbed stairs to the second floor, and found the old man bent over his desk in the land registration office.

"You talk to John Stone?" Brodbent asked.

"You look like you're gonna have a conniption fit, Jonas. What the hell's wrong?"

"What'd you tell him?"

"Go to the stamp mill."

Brodbent blew out the corner of his mouth. "Don't *ever* tell anybody about the stamp mill. John Stone's a newspaper reporter, trouble's his middle name. Anybody asks you again, the hills're full of gold."

"That were so, the whole world'd be here."

"That's the idea."

Rebecca sat on a stiff-backed unpadded wooden chair, the Bible balanced on her bony knees. *I held the crowd in the palm of my hand, but the devil's daughter bested me.*

The preacher lady dropped to her knees. *Why did you let it happen, God? What do you want of me?* She hadn't eaten all day, she was woozy, thirsty, but refused to surrender. God showed displeasure because she lusted for a man. *We're made perfect through suffering.*

She folded the Bible under her arm, headed for her bedroom. Curtains covered the windows, she undressed in the darkness. A thick leather belt studded with nails jutted into the flesh around her waist. She unfastened the buckle, a few rows of nails pulled away from her body, revealing scabs and festering pustules. Sucking in her stomach, she tightened the belt two notches, nearly fainting from constrictive pressure.

Barely able to breathe, she dropped her black dress over her head and buttoned the bodice. Pain washed up and down her body. She fell to her knees and whispered: "Thank you for the gift of your suffering, O Lord."

Patricia sat in her living room, crocheting a cat onto a pillowcase. *Should I go back to Maine? They'll say I couldn't keep my husband. Look how fat she got.*

Tempted toward the kitchen, she could choose between chicken, cake, leftover mashed potatoes, ham. Her mouth watered. She forced herself to remain seated, hefty legs visible in the folds of her skirt. The struggle was constant. Sometimes she won, sometimes she lost. To hell with it. Maybe some people need more food than others.

Gail and Patricia entered the hall corridor at the same moment. "I just had the most wonderful walk!" Gail declared. "What an interesting town! I even saw a riot in front of the Grand Palace, that place you told me not to go!"

"A riot? Was anybody hurt?"

"A miracle somebody wasn't killed." Gail walked into the living room, her cheeks flushed with emotion. "That woman Belle McGuinness was in the middle of it! I thought she was going to shoot a strange religious woman in a black dress, all she needed was a broomstick!"

"Miss Rebecca Hawkins, our local lunatic. In any other city in America, they'd have her in an asylum, but in Lodestone, she walks around like everybody else, ranting and raving. Why was Belle McGuinness going to shoot her?"

"Missed the first part. I think you're wrong about Belle McGuinness, Patricia. Never saw a woman like her. She was ready to take on the crowd. She would've *killed,* do you understand? She's a wonderful human being!"

Patricia collapsed onto a chair and buried her face in her hands. Gail sat beside her sister and placed her arm around Patricia's shoulders. "Are you all right?"

Even my kid sister's on the enemy's side. Patricia wiped her nose with a hankie.

"Momma used to say sometimes it's better if you tell someone," Gail reminded her.

"Bart's having a love affair with Belle McGuinness."

Gail stared wide-eyed at the far wall. She'd heard about things like this happening in the best of families, but not hers. "I'm sorry."

Patricia dabbed her eyes. "I guess I shouldn't blame Belle McGuinness. Maybe it's my fault, because I've become such a fat pig."

"It's *not* your fault. How long has Bart been seeing her?"

"Just found out recently. He buys her gifts."

"Get a divorce. You're still beautiful, Patricia. You could get married again. Lose a few pounds . . ."

Edgar Faraday hustled down the sidewalk, carrying his briefcase, stovepipe hat askew on his head. His breath came in short gasps and his chest felt tight, the usual symptoms accompanying the possible loss of advertising revenue.

Madden's bank advertised heavily in the *Lodestone Gazette,* and every time Madden formed a new company, its existence was announced with an ad. Faraday was anxious to clear up the mess, go on to the more rewarding task of publishing his crusading newspaper.

He arrived at the Lodestone Savings Bank. Madden sat behind his desk, puffing a cigar as he shuffled papers. "Have a seat."

Faraday dropped to a chair. Madden looked at him. "Fire John Stone."

"But he's the best reporter I've had in years."

Madden cringed beneath the compliment for his archrival.

"He asks too many questions, makes unfounded allegations, such as this region's tapped out."

Faraday turned on his old newpaperman's charm. "I decide what goes into the paper, Mr. Madden. You can be sure I'd never print any unfounded allegations. Besides, he has a second job. Manager of the Grand Palace Saloon. I fire him, he'll spend more time with Belle. You wouldn't want that, would you?"

Does everybody *know?* Madden thought. "Changed my mind. Give Stone more assignments, keep him busy. But if one disparaging remark about the economic prospects of this region ever appears in your newspaper, you'll end up on your obituary page."

"Lodestone is the fastest growing community in the Rockies," Faraday replied. "Chances are we'll be here after Denver's gone and forgotten. Now if you'll excuse me, I have a paper to get out."

Belle McGuinness paced her living room, scowling. She wore a black gown embossed with gold lion heads, hair piled high upon her head. Every time she passed the bottle of whiskey, she paused for a drink.

She thought of Rebecca Hawkins humiliating her in front of the whole town. The dirty-faced daughter of a whore cringed, afraid to go out and play because the other kids made fun of her.

She'd been terrified in front of the Grand Palace. *Crazy woman, dried-up old witch, can't take a walk without her jumping all over me.* Belle stamped her foot on the floor. *I know what she needs.*

Her hand trembled as she raised the glass to her bright red lips. Half in the bag, not even noon yet, because of that damned harpy. Belle dreaded seeing her again. *Afraid I'll kill the bitch.*

The triggers of the shotgun a tiny fraction from fire, I'd be the first woman in Lodestone to hang. It's frightening to lose control. If I see that woman again, God help both of us.

She carried the bottle and glass to the sofa and sat heavily on the cushions. *I can't hide in this goddamn building for the rest of my life, because of that prune. Can't put up with it any longer.*

She closed her eyes. The soft cushions swallowed her beautiful round behind. *I've come too far to let anybody get in my way.* She remembered the sad-faced little girl in a ragged dress, surrounded by taunting children throwing stones. A sob escaped from her throat. "She'll never do it to me again."

Patricia poured tea from a white glazed pot. On the other side of the low round table, Gail bit into an oatmeal cookie. "I forgot to tell you! I ran into that fellow John Stone, the former Confederate officer."

"The good-looking one?"

"In the space of one day, he's become manager of the Grand Palace Saloon! Can you imagine? He gave me a tour of the place."

Patricia stopped stirring her tea. "You went *inside* the Grand Palace?"

"He said it was safe, because killings usually happen only at night. You've heard the expression *den of iniquity*? That's exactly what it was. Filthy, dark, smelly, full of the dregs of humanity, but I felt safe with John Stone. I sort of invited him to dinner tonight. Would you rather he didn't come? I guess I have no right to invite people into your home."

"If you want him to come, it's all right with me."

"I'll go to the Grand Palace and leave a message."

"Don't ever chase a man. They won't respect you."

"John Stone's not like that."

"I think you've got a crush on him."

"Don't be silly. I hardly know the man. We're just friends, that's all."

"There's a messenger service we use. I'll show you how it works."

Patricia wrote the invitation, folded it, and put it into an envelope addressed to JOHN STONE. Gail followed Patricia to the back porch, a bell mounted on a wall. Patricia rang the clapper.

"Poor Negro children live in shacks on the other side of town," Patricia explained. "They run my errands."

Gail looked at hazy peaks on the horizon. "We think our Maine mountains are big, but they're foothills here. The West is an incredible immensity."

"See any injuns yet?"

"Sort of ratty, I thought."

"Kill you in a minute, and you won't even know what happened."

"Can't be worse than those robbers on the train. John Stone was the only man who stood up for me."

"He's brave or crazy. Sure you know which?"

"He's a real southern gentleman."

A small figure rounded the corner of a building straight ahead, running at top speed toward Gail and Patricia. He wore ragged clothes and patched boots, nappy black hair clipped short, face smudged with dirt,' he came to a stop in front of the porch. "Ma'am?"

Patricia handed him the envelope. "Give this to John Stone at the Grand Palace."

"What's he look like?"

"Real tall. He's the new manager."

"I'll find 'im, ma'am. You can count on me."

Patricia handed him a coin. "When you come back with his answer, I'll give you something to eat, all right?"

He ran away on skinny legs. The sisters returned to the living room. "I hope John Stone is free," said Gail.

"A bachelor will always accept a dinner invitation, because he knows he'll have a decent meal that night."

A gentleman in a dark suit crossed the lobby of the Crown Hotel in Denver. "Anything for me?" he asked the desk clerk.

"This just came in, Mr. LaFollette."

Randy LaFollette tucked the envelope into the inside pocket of his frock-coat jacket. He had a slim nose, black hair parted on the side, a mustache, one gold front tooth.

His room was silent and dark, cigar smoke and ladies' perfume permeated everything. He crossed to the window and pulled back the curtain, illuminating a black-tressed woman lying naked atop the bed. "You order breakfast?" she asked.

"I'd never let you go hungry, Amanda dear."

She rolled out of bed. He read the telegram, his face expressionless. Assignment in Lodestone.

"Going away again?" she asked nonchalantly.

"Not too far this time. Be home in a few days."

His face constructed of finely chiseled bones, his every movement bespoke elegance. She loved him, but he was a gunfighter. One day he'd come home in a box.

John Stone approached the big barnlike stamp mill. A face appeared in a window, sank out of sight. Rotted stumps everywhere, huge forests decimated to keep the mill running, terrific din, air full of acrid smoke. The secret to Lodestone was inside that building. He opened the door.

Six thick steel posts pounded up and down. A system of pulley and leather belts ran along the ceiling. In the middle of the floor, two rows of amalgamating pans with revolving mullers swished water mixed with pulverized ore. Workers pushed wheelbarrows, greased machinery, weighed minerals, wrote on notepads.

Something prompted Stone to look up. A sledgehammer fell toward him! He dived out of the way, the sledgehammer slammed into the floor where he'd stood. Another two seconds, he would have worn it for a hat.

A worker sat high in the rafters. "Sorry!"

Stone picked himself off the floor and dusted his clothes. A heavyset man with short red beard walked toward him.

"What can I do fer you?"

"Just wondering what quality of ore is coming through here."

"Highest grade."

"Mind if I take a look?"

"He'p yerself."

The foreman strolled away, but Stone didn't know what to look for. The air had a bitter chemical odor. Workers shook a fine shower of quicksilver into the amalgamating pans. Others added coarse salt and sulphate of copper. The steel stamps shook the building incessantly.

Stone asked a workman in a dirty apron: "How much gold you getting out of this ore."

"Talk to the boss." The man applied a wrench to a pipe joint beneath the pans. A thick jet of steam spewed at Stone, he dodged a moment before being scalded.

"Where's the boss?"

"Second floor."

Stone climbed the stairs, knocked on the door, turned the knob. Locked. He descended to the ground level, a group of workers formed below, carrying axes, hammers, a variety of tools.

A man nearly big as he, in a dirty leather apron and no shirt, massive hairy arms folded over his chest, stood at the bottom. Stone reached the last step.

"Get out of here," said leather apron.

"I'll leave when I'm ready."

Leather apron swung his fist at Stone's head. Stone ducked, then hooked a solid right to leather apron's jaw. Staggered, eyes rolling around in his head, the bulky man wondered what world he was in. Stone pushed him out of the way and headed for the door.

Rushing footsteps behind him, he spun around and pulled both Colts. They stopped in their tracks.

Stone backed to the door. Outside, a little Negro boy ran toward him. "You John Stone?"

The reporter read his dinner invitation, a faint smile formed. A genuine home-cooked meal after months of saloon and campfire cuisine. "Tell Miss Petigru I'll be happy to attend."

The boy ran down the hill. A shot rang out, ground exploded in front of Stone. He threw himself down, rolled over, came up with both Colts smoking, shattering windows in the stamp mill. Then he ran zigzag down the hill, dived behind an outcropping of rock, disappeared.

Men's and ladies' clothing hung in racks lining the walls of the haberdashery store. A stout man with a short black beard advanced toward John Stone. "Can I help you, signor?"

"Want to buy a suit."

The salesman appraised him like a jeweler with a gem. "You have money?"

"Put it on Belle McGuinness's account."

"My name is Luciano. This way, if you please."

Stone followed him to a full-length mirror. Luciano measured him with a tape. Stone looked at his reflection. *What would I think if I saw that coming at me?* He stood straighter, sucked in his stomach. Just another cowboy. "I have a dinner engagement at seven."

"Your suit will be ready at six, signor."

• • •

The little Negro boy pounded on the back door of the Madden home. The maid opened up. "What you want, boy?"

"I got a message frum . . ."

Gail slipped into the passageway. "I'll take care of this." She looked eagerly at the boy. "Did you find Mr. Stone?"

"Said he'd 'cept yer invitation. Can I eat now?"

They led him to the kitchen. The boy stared at piles of food. Gail made a thick roast beef sandwich and set it on the table. "You'll have to wash your hands first."

Dirt caked on his wrists and the back of his neck, his clothes practically nonexistent, the pathetic little waif washed his hands quickly in the basin on the counter, then semidried himself with a towel.

"Now?"

Patricia nodded. He pounced on the sandwich, stuffing it into his mouth. Patricia brought him a large glass of milk. Gail found ham left over from last night. Dolly placed a plate of apples and pears on the table. The cook brought bread and butter.

The boy chomped his way through everything in sight, his zeal and concentration wondrous to behold. Warm maternal feelings arose in the hearts of the women. They waited patiently until he finished. He drained the last drop of milk from the glass, leaned back in the chair, burped, and said, "A man needs ter fill his belly onc't in a while."

"Where's your mother?"

"Ain't got none."

"Where do you live?"

The boy shrugged.

"You don't have a roof over your head at night?"

The boy didn't like questions, but the nice ladies always asked. They didn't know how much it hurt to answer. "Guess I'll be movin' on," he said, raising himself laboriously from the chair. His belly stood out like the sixth month of pregnancy.

"What's your name?" asked Patricia, following him to the door.

"Tyrone."

"You don't have a family?"

He ran to the door, pulled it open, fled. Patricia stood

on the porch and held her palms near her mouth. "You get hungry, you come back here, understand?"

Belle sat before stacks of paper in her office, a glass of whiskey in her hand. "Where the hell've you been?" she said to John Stone. "Pull up a chair."

He sat beside her. *She continues at this pace, she'll be out like a light by sundown.*

"You got three things to do in that saloon." She slurred her words. "The first is make sure the bars're well stocked at all times. The second is make sure you got enough bartenders for every shift. The third is take care of any trouble that comes up. Want a drink?"

He shook his head.

"You're in charge of hirin' and firin' everybody on the first floor, and that includes the still. You been back there yet?"

"Don't even know where it is."

"You're an ex-Army officer. Thought it'd be the first place you'd go." She laughed at her joke, took another sip of whiskey.

Bad to drink early in the day, but Stone wouldn't preach to anybody. He awakened in too many shit piles.

"Din't I tell you to buy a suit?"

"I saw Luciano. The suit'll be ready tonight."

She smiled faintly. *I shouldn't be mean to him.* She touched the tip of her tongue to his ear. "I'm sorry if I'm a bad girl, but everything's a-goin' agin' me right now."

"I thought business was good."

"It ain't the business."

"Heard about you and the preacher woman. She's just another crackpot."

Belle opened a drawer and pulled out the gold-plated derringer. "Brought you a present."

The deadly little weapon fell into his palm. He read the inscription.

"Wear it around yer neck. Might come in handy someday. Somethin' to remember me by."

"I'd remember you without any present."

Something weakened inside her. "Let's go upstairs and get some grub."

• • •

Jamie Boggs ate his dinner in the kitchen, while Belle's cook sifted flour for a cake. Jamie's life was eternal silence, if not peace.

He worried about Belle, remembered the tension in her body as he carried her through the crowd. The religious woman hurt her deeply. She was extremely sensitive beneath her brazen exterior.

Formerly employed by the railroad, he happened to be in the cribs one night when a miner tried to kill Belle. He jumped in and pounded the miner into unconsciousness. She offered him a job. He'd been working for her ever since.

He worshiped her, loved to gaze at her face, felt privileged to serve her, would do anything for her, felt wonderful when she smiled and terrible when she was mad.

He wondered about John Stone. Was he using Belle? Stone spent the night with her, and Jamie didn't like to think about it. Stone seemed friendly enough, so did lots of bastards. If he ever hurts her, he'll die.

John Stone and Belle dined on roast lamb, potatoes, and string beans. A freshly baked loaf of bread sat on a block of wood, a knife sticking out. Stone cut two thick slices and passed one to Belle.

She watched him eat heartily. *Find out what he likes. The way to a man's heart is through his stomach, though some said the path was lower.* She poured another glass of whiskey.

"Something bothering you?" he asked.

"Shore ain't been my day. My maid quit this morning. Just disappeared. I got to find another one fast."

"Maybe she's sick."

"Would've said somethin'."

"Must be a reason. Things don't happen for nothing."

"I went lookin' for her this mornin', she was gone."

"When was the last time you saw her?"

"She was a-leadin' Marshal Kincaid to the door."

Stone's fork dangled in the air. "Maybe it's got something to do with Kincaid."

"I don't think they knowed each other."

"Where does she live?"

"Niggertown."

"Know her address?"

"White folks don't go to Niggertown. You go try it, you're liable not to git out alive."

A drunken miner passed out at the bar, another slept on the floor, a musician played an Irish fiddle on the stage.

Stone checked the liquor stock. In the kitchen, a Negro cook fried steaks at the stove. "Your dog ain't left since you been here last. Every now and then I throw him a piece of meat."

The hound gazed at Stone from the corner. Stone patted his head. "I wonder what his name is."

"That's just a soup hound," the cook said. "He don't get no name."

The dog looked up with pleading eyes at Stone. "You want a name?" Stone asked. "How about . . . Muggs?"

The dog barked.

"Muggs it is." Stone returned to the stove. "You know where Maxine Goines lives?" he asked the cook.

He shook his head no.

"She's Miss McGuinness's former maid. I want to talk with her."

"Don't know nothin' about it."

"Figured there aren't many of you people in town, you'd all know each other."

The cook flipped a steak in the air, caught it in the black greasy frying pan. "Us people don't all know each other."

"I'm going into your section of town to find her. You can't give me any idea where to look?"

"Wouldn't go there, I were you."

The stamp mill slammed in the distance. Muggs followed dutily along the sidewalk. A pack train of ore-laden mules trudged down the middle of the street. Stone and Muggs arrived at the *Lodestone Gazette*. Edgar Faraday looked up from his desk. "You've been causing me a lot of trouble, young man!"

Muggs growled, baring his fangs. Stone leaned his fists on Faraday's desk. "Start looking for another town to set up your printing press. Lodestone's on its way out."

"Where's your proof?"

"You can't prove there's gold here, and neither can anybody else. They tried to kill me at the stamp mill. How's that for a front-page story?"

"If I print it, no need to look for another town. I'll have a bullet in my head, but at least I won't have to worry about goddamned deadlines anymore. Don't you understand: This world's crooked from top to bottom. How many wars'll you have to fight before you figure it out?"

"What about decent folks being ruined? Shouldn't you warn them?"

"Give 'em a good story, that's what they like. There's one underneath your nose, but you haven't thought of it. The first three men to strike it rich in Lodestone live on the top floor of the Sheffield Hotel. They won't talk to me, but maybe they'll talk to you. People like to read about the rich and imagine themselves living in luxury too. You want to help the people of Lodestone, give them something to dream on. I'll pay an extra ten dollars for the story."

Stone left the *Lodestone Gazette,* followed by Muggs. A crowd of well-dressed people strolled on the far side of the street, somebody called his name. Mr. Moffitt, vice president of the Kansas Pacific Railroad, waved.

Stone crossed the street. Moffitt stood with his friends and associates, plus Mayor Ralston, members of the town council, and Marshal Kincaid, who glowered at Stone.

"You're still in town!" Mr. Moffitt said. "We were wondering what happened to you. Mayor Ralston, have you met John Stone?"

"Don't believe I have," said Mayor Ralston with a broad smile. Every adult a potential voter, he shook Stone's hand.

Moffitt chomped the cigar in the corner of his mouth and hooked his thumbs in his suspenders. "You may be interested to know John Stone's the man who shot . . . what's his name?"

"Tod Buckalew," offered one of the gentlemen.

Moffitt slapped John Stone on the shoulder. "I'd be honored if you'd come to my party tonight."

"I've already accepted a dinner invitation."

"Stop for a drink afterward. We're on the second floor of the Sheffield Hotel."

Stone made his way toward the outskirts of town, Muggs at his heels. Buildings became more decrepit, garbage lay in the gutters. An old white-haired Negro man drove a wagon down the middle of the street, mud sliding and dripping around the wheels. Stone saw Negro children playing on the sidewalk. They took one look at him and ran.

A young Negro woman, slim and pretty, stepped onto the sidewalk, carrying a basket on her arm. Her eyes widened when they fell on John Stone.

"I'm looking for Maxine Goines. You know where she lives?"

"You on the wrong side of town."

She scurried away. Dusky faces behind windows studied him. He could smell fear. Why'd Maxine Goines give up the best-paying maid job in Lodestone? Stone felt eerie in the silent neighborhood. A leader was somewhere in the community. They could reason together. Probably a lawyer or doctor. Look for his shingle.

Muggs padded behind him, growling in his throat. They heard a piano in the next building. No sign over the door, he pushed it open. The piano stopped. All conversation ceased. He approached the bar.

"Beer."

The bartender filled a glass. Stone tossed him a coin. "Know where I can find Maxine Goines?"

The bartender shook his head. The atmosphere could be cut with a knife. Stone sipped. The pianist returned to his keys, playing strange rhythms. Stone felt like an intruder. He placed the half-full mug of beer on the bar and walked outside.

Muggs waited for him. A brightly painted barber's pole grew on the far side of the street, next to a window revealing a Negro getting a haircut. Stone turned the corner and saw a small sign:

CHURCH
Reverend Jack Reynolds

Stone crossed the street and knocked on the door. A wizened Negro woman opened it.

"Want to speak with your pastor."

"What for?"

A Negro man in black suit and white collar appeared in the vestibule. He was in his thirties and wore thick spectacles. "May I help you?"

"I was looking for Reverend Reynolds."

"That's me—how do you do?"

They shook hands. Reynolds was an educated man. Stone felt at ease. "I wondered if I could ask you a question."

"Delia, bring us some tea."

Reynolds led Stone to a small room with a desk and jam-packed bookshelves. A plain empty cross nailed to the wall, the inscription read: HE IS RISEN.

"What can I do for you?"

"I'm looking for Maxine Goines." Stone explained how she'd left Belle McGuinness's employ under mysterious circumstances. "Could you take me to her?"

"No, because it would place her in jeopardy."

"From whom?"

"You're new in town, but you've already become Belle McGuinness's latest lover, new reporter for the *Lodestone Gazette,* and you push into places you don't belong."

Stone was surprised. "How do you know all that?"

"We wash your floors, cook your food, take care of your children. We know everything that happens in your part of town."

"Did Marshal Kincaid threaten Maxine Goines?"

"Mind your business, you want to keep living."

"I'm sure somebody told Christ to mind his business, but he didn't."

"You're not Christ."

"Neither are you."

Silence for a few moments, the maid brought in a pot of tea with two cups, served the hot green liquid, backed out of the room. Reverend Reynolds stirred his tea.

"They say you're a gunfighter, Mr. Stone. I'm sure you can defend yourself against anybody, but what about Maxine, and what about me?"

"Maybe I'd better go."

"You may finish your tea. The damage has already been done."

"I'm sorry . . ."

"Some people like to stir things up, peek underneath rocks, go where they shouldn't."

"This town's going bust, but nobody believes it. Investors stand to lose their life savings in worthless stock."

"No one in this part of town has anything to invest or lose."

"When the bubble bursts, everyone will be hurt. Could be riots. It's happened before."

"We've survived worst. If you want to worry, better worry about yourself, Mr. Newspaper Man. The people who run this town won't tolerate you long. A miracle you haven't been killed already. My advice to you: Get on the next train."

Stone ambled through the central business district of Lodestone. Something crashed onto his shoulder, the hand of Kevin McGeachy. "Heerd you moved in with Belle McGuinness. When you a-gonna invite me fer dinner?"

Stone eyed McGeachy with new interest. The miner dug earth every day, a prime source of firsthand information about what was in the ground. "You found gold in your mine yet?"

"Once I get below the ledge I'm on now, hit the mother lode."

"You ever actually meet anybody who struck gold?"

"Lots of 'em."

"Name one."

"Them three fellers livin' on the top floor of the Sheffield."

"Anybody else?"

"What you drivin' at?"

"What if this town's a hoax? What if the mines never were?"

"Couldn't be."

"Why not?"

"I'd shoot myself, I believed that."

"Sell the Grand Monarch while you still can. Get the hell out of here."

"Sometime you give a man a pain in the ass. See you later at the Grand Palace."

They don't want to know the truth. Faraday was right. Something drew Stone's attention to the far side of the street. Underneath the eaves, walking along slowly, Marshal Kincaid glared at him. *He knows that I know,* Stone thought. *Maybe we should have a talk. About what? I know you're an outlaw? Keep walking. Stay out of his way, hope he stays out of mine.*

The train bells rang and whistle blew. "All aboard for Kansas and points east!"

A Negro porter carried Randy LaFollette's valise toward the stairs to the railway car. "Should be home by Sunday," he said to Amanda. "Assignment's not far away."

Amanda LaFollette forced a smile, though she felt queasy in her stomach. "Getting cold," she said. "Don't forget to wear your sweater."

He took her in his arms. "Just remember I love you."

She kissed his lips. "Be careful."

"Last call for Kansas and points east! Aboooarrrd!"

They parted, he ran to the stairs. A conductor waited, examining his fob watch. The bell on the engine clanged. LaFollette entered the parlor car. Two Negro men in white coats served drinks to an assortment of travelers. LaFollette waved good-bye to his wife through the window. She blew him a kiss as the train pulled out of the station.

He hung his Louisiana planter's hat on a peg, pulled off his doeskin gloves, sat at a table. Lodestone in three hours. He leaned back and lit a cheroot. A Negro waiter took his order. He thought of Amanda worrying about him. She dragged his mind, interfered with his concentration, but he loved her, needed her, couldn't get along without her.

He met her in Muncie, Indiana, the schoolmaster's daughter. She combined a country girl's wholesome loving heart with a good education in the classics, deserved better than a gunfighter, his life awash in blood, but God brought them together and made her his woman.

The waiter served whiskey. *Better off single,* Randy LaFollette mused. *Concentrate better. But I'd be lonely. Drink too much. Get killed anyway.*

Raised in Delaware, son of a lawyer, expelled from numerous academies of learning, black sheep of his family, he had no respectable profession. Once, a long time ago, he shot a gambler over the turn of a card. Then somebody hired him to gun down a business rival. One assignment led to another. An old-timer told him he had talent. He practiced assiduously, invested in Denver real estate, got married, settled down. Life was good.

An elderly gentleman and lady approached the next table. "Do you mind?" he asked LaFollette.

"By all means."

They sat beside him. "Charles Johnston, and this is my wife, Vivian."

LaFollette told them his name.

The gentleman had a big white mustache, his wife's hair matched his. "What business are you in, if you don't mind me asking, Mr. LaFollette?"

"Death."

Mr. Johnston and his wife paled in the wan morning light.

"I sell equipment and supplies to undertakers."

Johnston smiled, thankful to be back in the business world again. "You must see a lot of the country. What's your favorite town?"

"Denver, where I live."

"We're on our way to Ohio. Own a small factory there that makes hardware. Your firm might use our tools to make coffins. How's business these days?"

"I expect it to pick up shortly."

7

MADDEN HUNG HIS hat in the vestibule. He didn't want to face Patricia and her sister, but a banker ate supper with his family. Patricia wanted a real husband and real marriage, as if such things existed. A grouchy expression on his face, he made his way to the living room. Patricia and Gail sat on chairs facing each other before the fireplace, light aureoling around them. He bent to kiss his wife's cheek.

"Don't touch me," she said icily.

He poured a shot of whiskey. Nonchalant and suave on the outside, steaming internally, he asked: "Well, what have you ladies done today?"

Neither spoke. *They've formed a cabal against me.* "Did you take a walk through town, Gail? See anything interesting?"

"The riot."

Belle McGuinness was the center of the riot, and everyone knew which errant husband was sleeping with her. *My wife hates me, Belle's giving me the runaround, and people say the gold's gone. What worse thing could happen to me today?*

"By the way," Patricia said, "we're having a dinner guest tonight."

Madden brightened. "Who?"

"Gentleman named John Stone."

91

Madden's glass of whiskey dropped out of his hand and went crashing to the floor. Shards of glass flew in all directions.

"Are you all right, dear?" Patricia asked, a sly smile on her face.

"My suit ready?"

Luciano rubbed his hands together. "Of course, sir. Right this way, sir." He led Stone to a row of suits on hangers and pulled one down. "Try it on."

Stone stepped behind the curtain and donned his new suit. Then he stood before the mirror. A strange dude stared at him in shock. *I look like the lawyer who just bribed the judge. I can't wear this goddamn thing.*

"How you like it?" Luciano asked proudly.

"Fits real well," Stone replied. Can't hurt the man's feelings. "While I'm here, want to get a regular pair of pants and a shirt. Could also use a good wool sweater."

Stone returned to the closet and put on his regular clothes. Luciano laid out the merchandise on the counter. Stone selected black jeans, butternut shirt, red sweater. "Put in on Miss McGuinness's account."

He left the haberdashery store and paused at the first alley. Halfway down lay a drunkard with an empty bottle in his right hand. Stone dropped the suit beside him, then returned to the street, entered the Grand Palace Saloon.

A few blocks away Marshal Kincaid slowed as he approached the bootmaker's shop. In front of it, on the planked sidewalk, sat a Negro with a glass eye. "Shine you up, Marshal?"

"Don't mind if I do."

Kincaid sat on the stool. The bootblack worked both brushes against the leather covering Kincaid's toes. Kincaid looked to his left and right, then filled his pipe with tobacco.

"You hear anythin' 'bout the girl?" Kincaid asked in a low tone.

The bootblack didn't look up at him. "She's still home, 'fraid to come out. You ain't gonna hurt her, is you, Marshal?"

"Got better things to do than shoot dumb little pickaninnies."

"Somethin' happened today, you oughtta know 'bout. John Stone was in our part of town lookin' fer Maxine Goines, but din't find her. Had a little talk with Reverend Reynolds, and left. Ain't been back since."

Marshal Kincaid's teeth grinded the bit of his pipe.

Madden sat in a corner of the living room, listening to Patricia and Gail talking about Bangor, Maine, ignoring him as if he didn't exist. Put rat poison in John Stone's food? Bart played with the idea, but Stone might taste the chemicals and go for his guns. Randy LaFollette was on his way to Lodestone, better let him handle it.

Madden's mind produced business schemes of every type. His father, a traveling salesman, encouraged him in this vein even when Bart was small. He learned his lessons well, arrived in Lodestone at the crucial moment, built a fortune, now worried about losing everything, including Belle.

"How do you know this John Stone fellow?" he asked Gail. "Where did you meet him?"

"On the train. When the robbers tore my clothes, he came to my aid."

"What does he do for a living?"

"I believe he's a cowboy."

"Not much money in that. See gentlemen on your own social level, if you don't mind a little good-intentioned brotherly advice. What's he doing in Lodestone?"

"The outlaws took all his money. He found work at the Grand Palace."

Patricia smiled at her husband. "You know all about the Grand Palace, don't you, dear?"

"Everybody knows the Grand Palace, dear."

"I understand they have prostitutes."

"Most saloons do."

"You ever met Belle McGuinness?"

"A few times."

"They say she has many male admirers. You know everything that goes on in this town, Bart. Tell us about her."

Bart mopped his brow with his handkerchief. "You might be interested to know that our supper guest, John Stone, is living with her."

Gail's jaw dropped. "You can't be serious!"

"It's what people say." He glanced meaningfully at his wife. "But you know how harmful gossip can be."

Gail felt a twinge in her breast. John Stone and Belle McGuinness?

John Stone lay in the bathtub, eyes closed, cigarette dangling from his lips. Hot soapy water washed filth and scabs away from his battered body. He puffed his cigarette. The new maid filled his glass with freshly made lemonade, then retired silently.

Stone looked out the window at the clear blue sky. Belle appeared in the doorway. The setting sun made a halo around her head, she wore a frilly black gown. One hand carried a cigarette, the other a whiskey glass.

"Look who's home," she said in her offhand sarcastic tone. "How's the saloon?"

"Fine last time I looked."

"There's somethin' I want you to do." She pulled a string, her gown fell away from her body. "Make room."

She crawled into the tub with him, her body smooth and slippery. Mad lust overwhelmed him. He squeezed her tightly, pressed his lips against hers. Waves of suds rolled back and forth endlessly.

Kincaid walked into his house. His wife bent over the stove in the kitchen.

"Look what the cat drug in," she said.

He sat at the table. "What's fer supper?"

"Beef stew and biscuits."

One of his favorites. He refilled his corncob pipe. "Get me a glass of whiskey."

She opened the cupboard and pulled down a quart of Rocky Mountain Fine Blended. "Somethin' botherin' you?" she asked. "You can't hide yer moods from me, y'know. Found another woman?"

"Can't even handle you, never mind another woman."

She placed the bottle and glass in front of him. He poured three fingers of whiskey.

"Too bad Belle McGuinness didn't shoot the preacher lady today," said Dolly. "Who's she to tell other folks how to live?"

Kincaid's mind was elsewhere. If John Stone went to

Niggertown to talk with Maxine Goines, he was on Kincaid's trail. *Where the hell's Randy LaFollette?*

Stone shaved before the mirror, towel wrapped around his waist, barefoot. Belle sat on the sofa, sipped her glass of whiskey.

"You ever been to San Francisco, Belle?"

"I been everywhere. You know that, Johnny."

"What can you tell me about the place?"

"Half the people're thieves and murderers. You can git killed any time of the day or night, even in yer own hotel room. You won't like it. The wide-open spaces for a man like you."

"You read me like a book, Belle."

"I know men. Met a million of 'em."

"Tell me more about San Francisco."

"To hell with San Francisco. Start yer ranch, if that's what you wanna do. We could be partners, fifty-fifty. I'll take care of the business end, you handle cattle operations."

Silence fell over the room. *If I say yes, I'd get everything I want, except Marie.* "Can't do it, Belle. You know I'm engaged. But I appreciate the offer. Maybe someday, who knows, might take you up on it."

"Offer might not be good then." She sipped whiskey, tried not to be hurt. He put on his new cowboy outfit. "Where's the suit I asked you to git?"

"Can't wear it. Felt like a goddamned idiot, or the kind of man who'd embezzle public funds."

"When I tell you to do something, I 'spect it to git done."

"The saloon downstairs is running like a clock. That's the main thing."

"I'll decide what's the main thing. My manager wears a goddamned suit. This ain't no bust-out whoop and holler."

"Don't wear suits. Sorry."

Blood rose to her face. She didn't come this far to let some dumb cowboy tell her how to run her business. "That's the way you feel about it, you're fired!"

She saw the hurt on his face. He gathered his things silently. "I'll give you the money for the suit soon as I get paid."

"Don't want yer goddamned money. Where's the suit now? Maybe Luciano can cut it down for Jamie."

"I gave it to a bum in an alley."

The humor of the situation struck her. She imagined a drunkard staggering around in an expensive suit too big for him. *What the hell do I care about a suit? Johnny looks like a little boy what just got spanked.* "Didn't mean it, cowboy. You know how I git sometimes. Come over here and give momma a kiss." He didn't move. She arose from the sofa. "I said I'm sorry. Can't you forgive Belle when she's bad?"

They kissed. He thought of Marie. *What'm I doing?*

"What's wrong?" she asked.

"Got to get moving. Been invited to supper with the Madden family."

"I thought you were havin' supper with me."

"You never said anything about it before."

"How'd you wrangle the invite?"

"Gail Petigru sent it to me out of the blue. I met her on the train yesterday. She's Mrs. Madden's sister from Bangor, Maine."

"How old is she?"

"Maybe eighteen."

Belle's temper flowed warm. "Say hello to Bart Madden for me. He's a *friend* of mine."

"What the hell's that supposed to mean?"

"Just what you think. We used to screw, to say it in plain English." She smiled grimly at the jealousy and pain that distorted his face.

The train snaked its way around an immense mountain, stars twinkled in the sky. Randy LaFollette sat alone in the dining car, chewing a chicken sandwich, concentration increased, muscles tensed, eyes sharpened. He sped toward the killing ground, anticipated the instant he'd pull the trigger, a fiery flash, like the penultimate moment of love.

He wondered who his victim would be this time. Usually somebody's hired gun, or a love rival, business partner gone sour, somebody's husband, somebody's brother, LaFollette saw them all fall before his smoking gun.

Probably sitting down to supper right now. Hope he enjoys

it. Tomorrow morning I'll catch the first train back to Denver.

John Stone stepped onto the porch of the Madden home, new pants tucked into boots cavalry style, two Colts tied to his legs. His knuckles rapped against the door, opened by a Negro maid. She knows everything that goes on in this home, and so does everyone in the Negro district.

"You must be Mr. Stone," the maid said, accepting his old Confederate hat.

Gail entered the vestibule and looked like she'd bitten a lemon. She introduced him to her sister. Bart stood beside the bar nonchalantly, measuring Stone. *A gunfighter if ever I saw one.* They shook hands firmly. Stone sat on a chair. The maid brought a glass of wine imported from the Loire Valley. Bart's smile a little too polished, Stone took an instant dislike to him. Bart thought Stone a drifter, liar, and seducer of unsuspecting women.

"Saw you coming up the walk," Bart said. "That a rebel hat you wore? Trying to prove something?"

"When it wears out, I'll throw it away."

"You believe in slavery?"

"I believe this town's gone bust, but doesn't know it. If I owned the biggest bank, I'd unload all assets immediately for whatever I could get."

"What makes you think this town's gone bust?"

"There's no gold."

"Just because you haven't found any, doesn't mean it's gone."

"Nobody else found any either for a long time."

"Tell that to the prospectors who've taken millions from these mountains."

"What prospectors?"

Patricia interrupted: "I hate business talk. Leave it at the office, would you, Bart?" She averted her glance to her dinner guest. "I understand you work for Belle McGuinness. Is she as wicked as everyone says?"

Stone saw her in the bathtub, splashing soapsuds onto the floor. "In what way?"

"It's a house of prostitution, isn't it?"

He stuttered. Bart enjoyed his discomfort, while Gail felt

sorry for him. *He must hate me for inviting him here.*

"Yes, there's prostitution," Stone admitted.

"It doesn't bother you to work in such a place?"

"Got to earn a living somehow."

"One would think a gentleman would get an *honest* job."

Gail rose to her feet. "I think it's disgusting what you're doing! Blaming him for what Belle McGuinness does!"

Silence in the living room, Bart coughed into his hand. John Stone gulped wine.

"We're being rude," Patricia said. "I'm sorry."

"All families have disagreements," Stone replied, rising from his chair. "Perhaps I'd better let you carry this one on without me. The best of luck to all of you in the coming crash of this town."

He was on his way to the vestibule before anyone could say anything. Gail placed her hand on his arm. "Please don't be angry with me. I didn't know my brother-in-law and you are . . . sleeping with Belle McGuinness."

"I'm not angry at you."

"I believed you when you said you were searching for the woman you love."

"I am."

"How can you sleep with Belle McGuinness?"

"I don't know." He appeared embarrassed.

"I wasn't trying to accuse you of anything. I thought you were one kind of person, and you're not."

Stone held her shoulders in his hands. "If I were you, I'd go back to Bangor. The lid's about to blow off this town, and I'm not kidding."

He kissed her lightly on the forehead. When she opened her eyes, he was on his way back to the center of town.

"Sit down," Belle ordered Jamie Boggs. "Something I want you to do."

He dropped to the sofa beside her, read her lips as she spoke.

"Get a jug of coal oil and some rags. Bring them here, and don't let anybody see what you've got. We're a-gonna set a little fire."

He shook his head vigorously, made inarticulate sounds of protest.

"We won't get caught," she said. "That bitch'll never point her finger at me again!"

She pushed him out the door, then poured another glass of whiskey. Her mood grew darker with every passing moment.

John Stone entered the opulent lobby of the Sheffield Hotel. Well-dressed gentlemen and ladies milled about, fire crackled in the stone hearth. A candlelit dining room on the right, he veered toward the stairs. Polished wood and brass elegance were everywhere. A muscular gentleman in a suit stepped before him.

"May I ask where you're goin', sir?"

"Mr. Moffitt's party."

"Your name?"

"John Stone."

Heads spun around. Belle McGuinness's man. The clerk checked a list of names. "Suite two-eighteen, sir."

Stone climbed the stairs. A Negro gentleman in a white jacket opened the door. He entered a fashionably appointed suite full of people in formal evening clothes. In the corner, a man sat on a stool and played Mozart on his violin.

Stone was the only one dressed like a cowboy, armed with two Colts, a knife sticking out of each boot.

"What's *that*?" asked one of the ladies.

Moffitt stepped forward, holding out his hand. "Glad to see you, Johnny. Can I get you something to drink?"

"Whatever you're having."

"Let me introduce you to some people." Moffitt dragged him by the arm into the room. "This is the fellow I've been telling you about, John Stone."

They stared at Stone as if he were from Mars. "Is he the one who shoots people?" asked Mrs. Winthrop, early forties, wearing a topaz heart pinned to the front of her chiffon gown.

"Where did you get that?" he asked.

"Why do you ask?"

"It's very beautiful."

She unpinned it from her bosom. "It's yours."

The bauble fell into his hand. "You're very generous, madam."

"Everything I do," she replied, "I do for a reason." She had faint streaks of gray in her hair, fine features, foxy eyes.

"Could you tell me where you got it?"

"Jewelry store down the street."

Everyone stared at the strange man in their midst. His eyes found a table groaning beneath platters of steaks, vegetables, poultry prepared several ways, three types of bread, pot of rare belugan caviar. He hadn't seen such a feast since they burned old Dixie down.

"Excuse me," he said.

The ladies and gentlemen from the East watched as he made his way toward the table. "Cuts quite a figure, doesn't he?" asked Mrs. Winthrop.

"Just another tall tale looking for a free meal," her husband replied.

Stone lay a massive turkey leg on his plate, followed with a slice of prime ribs, a length of Italian sausage, a baked potato drenched with cow butter.

"He's certainly hungry," said Mrs. Winthrop.

Another gentleman added: "I wouldn't want to tangle with him."

"I would," whispered Mrs. Winthrop.

"What was that?" her husband asked.

"Only clearing my throat, dear."

Stone carried food to an empty round table covered with a white tablecloth. A waiter poured a goblet of champagne. He lay the napkin on his lap, picked up his fork, gazed at the food. *What should I try first?*

He plunged the fork into sauteed mushrooms. The nearly forgotten taste carried him back to his father's dining-room table, the last place he'd eaten mushrooms. Marie sat to his right, her hand innocently on his lap, always touching.

A tidal wave of immeasurable soul-sickness rolled over him. *I'll follow you to the ends of the earth. You'll never get away from me. If you're dead, I'll dig up your grave and pull it in over me. I'll find you no matter what it costs or how long it takes. You'll never escape me.*

He looked up from his mushrooms. Mrs. Winthrop sat opposite him. "Who are you?" she asked. "I don't mean your name. I remember what it is. You're John Stone. But who are you?"

He dug into the food, a big swashbuckling ex-Army officer

in civilian clothes, wearing heavy guns, ignoring her question.

"Who was Tod Buckalew?" she asked.

Stone shrugged, kept eating.

"Why'd you kill him?"

He bit into the turkey leg. Her eyes roved over his shoulders and chest. He ate as if starved, golden hair gleaming in the light of lamps.

Her voice dropped an octave, she leaned an elbow on the table. "You're an extraordinary man, you know that?"

"In what way?" he asked, because he considered himself a failure.

She opened her mouth, no words came. *What is it?* she asked herself. She'd met big men before, men with good manners, and men much more handsome than John Stone. *What does he have?* She couldn't pinpoint it, but it had something to do with the ease with which he moved, a certain insouciant self-assurance, steady as the north star, a bit of the lost little boy. "You wouldn't understand," she said.

Moffitt blew a cloud of tobacco out the side of his mouth. "Understand what?"

"We were talking about Tod Buckalew," she replied.

"What about him?"

"I asked Mr. Stone why he killed him."

Both of them looked at John Stone, expecting an answer. He swallowed and said, "Self-defense."

Moffitt wanted to press the issue, but something said *don't do it.* "How do you like Lodestone?"

"Not much."

"Why don't you leave?"

"They cleaned me out in the robbery. Had to find a job."

Mrs. Winthrop turned to Moffitt. "Why can't he travel with us? There are spare berths."

Rich men don't give things away, but Moffitt found two reasons in Stone's favor: His Colts slung low and tied down. "If you'd like to continue as our guard, I'll pay your salary all the way to San Francisco."

"Can't leave my pard."

Moffitt recalled the disreputable old bum who traveled with Stone, wondered whether to call off the deal. Stone perceived Moffitt's resistance. "If you're interested in authentic western characters, you can't get much more authentic than Slipchuck," he said, huckstering his old saddle buddy. "He's been everywhere, done everything, a walking history book of the frontier. Don't sell him short by the way he looks. Put him in a clean suit of clothes, he'd be your dear old grandfather."

Moffitt pondered the proposition. If the train broke down, or a bridge washed out, they might have to fight Shoshonis. "It's a deal."

Several blocks away, Jonas Brodbent knelt in front of his safe, twirling the dial. On the other side of his desk sat Amos Twimby, a gnome with scruffy reddish-brown hair. Brodbent pulled a burlap bag out of his safe and placed it on his desk. "Take a look."

Twimby reached inside the bag and pulled out a rock laced with yellow lines. "The real stuff."

Brodbent leaned toward him. "You get caught, you don't know me, and I don't know you."

"Ain't never snitched on nobody a-fore."

"The Western Sovereign Mine at Sagamore Lake. Just drop it in the bottom and get the hell out of there. Make sure you don't wake anybody up."

"I know how to do it," Twimby aid with a conspiratorial wink. "This ain't me first time, remember?"

Stone looked up the stairs where three millionaires lived. *Ten more dollars if I write a good story. Need every penny when I get to San Francisco.* He climbed the stairs. A guard sat with a double-barreled shotgun cradled on his lap.

"I'm from the *Lodestone Gazette,* like to talk with the gentlemen up here."

The guard raised the shotgun and beckoned down the stairs. "Get going."

Stone kicked the shotgun out of his hands, the triggers tripped by mistake. Both barrels exploded, the corridor filled with smoke, hundreds of tiny pellets sprayed the ceiling. The guard fell to the carpet, rolled over, came up gun in hand.

Stone fired his Colt, the gun flew out of the guard's hand, the corridor echoed with the explosion. The guard blinked. He still wasn't sure what happened. A nearby door opened, revealing a man in long underwear, a shotgun in his hands. "What the hell's goin' on out here!"

"I'm from the *Lodestone Gazette,* and I wonder if I could ask you a few questions, sir."

"Don't talk to newspapers. Down the steps, or I'll put a hole in you that a wagon could ride through."

"You know what they say? You're a crazy skinflint son of a bitch. Here's your chance to give your side of the story."

"What do I care what they say? I can buy and sell the whole damned bunch of 'em! Don't give a damn either way. I ain't lookin' fer favors. Once a man gits money, everybody tries to take it from him. Can't walk the sidewalk without parasites askin' me fer handouts. Every mother's son got a charity, investment, sad story. Never leave a man alone. You think it's easy bein' rich? Well, it ain't. You got to invest wisely. One company goes out of business, two more come into being. Jay Gould and his gang in New York buy and sell each other every day. The economy's a rubber ball. They bounce it up and down whenever it suits them, but they can't fool me. I'll outsmart 'em, 'cause I understand their game."

"What was it like when you struck gold?"

"That was Lemuel what found the gold. You'd better ask him. My name's Jacob Sloat."

"John Stone."

"Heard that name before. Ain't you Belle McGuinness's new fancy man? Used to be one of her best customers. Really knows how to shake that ass, don't she?"

Sloat pounded on the nearest door with the butt of his shotgun. A short man with a long beard, wearing a black evening suit, white shirt, and diamond stickpin in his bright red cravat, greeted them.

"Who's this galoot?" Lemuel asked suspiciously.

Sloat made the introduction. "He wants to know what happened when you hit paydirt?"

"None of his goddamn business."

Sloat held up his hands to Stone apologetically. "Lemuel ain't the friendliest person in the world."

"What the hell I have to be friendly fer?" Lemuel declared. "What anybody do fer me? Worked hard for all I got. You'd think we're millionaires!"

"You're not?" Stone asked.

"Never was that much ore. I'll show you somethin'."

He led them into his deluxe suite of rooms. On a desk near the fireplace were several stacks of gold coins. "This is all I got left," he said. "Thirty thousand dollars. We only divided 'bout a hundred thousand 'twixt us in the beginning, ain't that right, Jacob?"

"He's right," Sloat said, "but I ain't cryin' poor mouth. I invested my money wisely. A company in New York's workin' on a machine that'll let you talk to somebody in another town. Company in New Jersey figuring out how to light lamps with wire and air."

"Bosh," said Lemuel. "Pie in the sky. The onliest thing that really matters is gold. Love to touch the stuff." He fingered his coins, lost in thought.

"He sits there all day and half the night," Sloat said as he led Stone to the door. "Stacks and restacks gold coins. Sometimes he'll put one in his mouth and suck like candy. Gold can make a man crazy."

"Where's the third partner?"

"Really gone bonkers, that one." He led Stone to the door, turned the knob. The room was dark except for one lone candle still burning in a holder.

Stretched out on the bed was a naked obese man with a long beard. On either side of him, also stupefied, naked women, bottles strewn across the floor, a table of food half-eaten, clothes lying everywhere, stench of whiskey and tobacco.

"That man was skinny as me once," Sloat said. "A sober, steady, hard-working miner. Soon as he got his hands on money, drinkin' and whorin' ever since. He'll kill himself he keeps on this way, but he can't stop. Maybe he'll run out of money first."

Stone descended the stairs. Had the Grand Monarch been salted? For one hundred thousand dollars, a smart man could make millions.

Slipchuck pushed his broom down the second-floor corridor, a new red bandanna tied round his neck. Jamie grunted, beckoned with his head.

"What the hell you want?" Slipchuck asked.

Jamie grabbed his shirt and pulled him to the stairs.

Slipchuck climbed to the third floor behind him. *Must be a special sweeping job,* Slipchuck thought happily. *Maybe I can git a peep at the boss lady takin' her bath.*

Slipchuck found himself in the living room of Belle's apartment. The boss lady sat on the sofa, wearing a low-cut black gown and a pearl necklace, a red rose affixed to her hair. "Have a seat, you old codger. I want to palaver with you."

Slipchuck dropped to a chair. Belle filled her glass half full of whiskey and handed it to him. *The boss lady is a-tryin' to git into my pants,* he thought happily. He winked, like the young stagecoach driver he'd been so long ago.

"You got somethin' in yer eye?" She threw him a hankerchief.

He touched it to his nose. Her perfume intoxicated him.

"Tell me 'bout John Stone."

"What yer want to know?"

"He got a girl in every town?"

"Ain't my place to say."

"Got his pick, ain't he?"

"Damned if I know."

"A man like John Stone needs a woman to take care of him."

"He'll git shot a-fore long," Slipchuck mused. "I can see it a-comin'. Sometimes a man's got to back down, but not John Stone. Goes plumb loco when somebody starts a-pushin' on him. Never seen nothin' like it."

"You're his pard. He'd listen to you." She leaned forward, breasts nearly falling out of her bodice. "How'd you like to sleep with a different whore every night for the rest of your life? You git John Stone to settle down here with me, take yer pick of the girls. He'd never have to worry again, and neither would *you,* old man."

They heard noise in the hall. Slipchuck opened the door. Jamie Boggs scuffled with Bart Madden.

"Get your goddamn hands off me!" Madden hollered indignantly. "I'll sue!"

"What the hell're you doin' here?" Belle asked Madden.

The banker straightened the front of his suit. "Had to talk with you, Belle."

"Must be serious, a-comin' to the Grand Palace where folks can see you. Ain't you afraid of yer reputation?"

"That's what I want to talk with you about."

"Take a walk," she said to Slipchuck. "You too," to Boggs.

Boggs muttered malevolently at Madden. She closed the door behind them. Madden spotted the bottle of whiskey. "Been drinking, Belle?"

She flopped onto the sofa and poured another glass. "So what if I have?"

"I'm going to divorce my wife, marry you just the way you wanted."

"You're a week too late. Got another man."

"John Stone? He's a saddle tramp."

"Lodestone's goin' bust, accordin' to him."

"That stupid hat he wears around. Probably wasn't even in the war."

"I seen war wounds before. He got 'em all over his poor body. I think he's an honest man, unlike some I've met."

Madden's smile faltered as he thought of them naked in bed together. "He'll leave you in the lurch, mark my words."

"Like you're a-leavin' yer wife?"

"That's different!"

"I wouldn't trust you as far as I could throw you, Bart."

His face flushed with shame, he made a threatening motion. She pulled up her dress and slipped out her derringer. "I'll blow yer goddamned head off."

He stared down the twin barrels. "Look at us, Belle. We're ready to kill each other. Everything was all right before that damned John Stone came to town. But he won't be around long."

"Is he leaving?"

Madden laughed snidely, recalling Randy LaFollette. "In a manner of speaking."

"What're you sayin'?"

He let the cat out of the bag, now had to stuff it back. "Drifters don't stay in one place long. After he moves on, what'll you do?"

"I saved my money, and not in yer crooked bank either. All a woman needs is a roof over her head. Men're a headache. If they're not a-lyin' to one woman, they're a-lyin' to 'nother."

● ● ●

Jamie Boggs smoked a cigarette nervously. He'd never seen Belle in such a state. She drank nearly a quart bottle of whiskey that day. Tougher than a man one moment, a child the next. Boggs loved her madly and hopelessly, wanted to take care of her, but he was a deaf mute, object of pity and derision.

He pounded his fist on the table, cursing his infirmity. *If only I was like other men. Maybe someday she'll see me for what I really am.* He saw an old Confederate cavalry hat coming up the stairs, gurgled as he rushed out the door, shaking his head no.

"What's wrong?" Stone asked, reaching for the doorknob.

Jamie made guttural sounds and waved his hands frantically. He pointed to Belle's door and shook his head. Stone pushed the door open, saw Belle facing Bart Madden in the middle of an argument.

Belle, white as a sheet, unsteady on her feet, spilled whiskey from the glass in her hand. Her fierce expression transformed into a smile.

"You two know each other?"

Madden wore no visible guns, but surely had one stashed somewhere. Stone watched his hands. "I visited Mr. Madden and his lovely wife earlier in the evening."

Madden choked with jealousy and rage. He opened his mouth but couldn't speak. Stone behaved as if he could do anything. Take him down a peg in front of Belle.

"The gentleman visited my home this evening," he explained, "to pay court to my young sister-in-law. How many female admirers do you have in this town, Mr. Stone?"

Belle looked accusingly at Stone. He raised his hands in the air. "She invited me to supper and I went. She's a friend of mine. We got robbed together on the train yesterday."

"Not the way I heard it," Madden said. "I have reason to believe you're attempting to seduce my sister-in-law, who's practically a child."

"Your whole life is a deception," Stone replied. "I know a flimflam man when I see one. Go home to your wife. I want to talk with Belle."

She looked at the banker. "Get the hell out of here."

Madden was stunned. "After all that's happened between us, you're treating me like your servant!" He poked his thumb into his chest. "This is Bart Madden you're talking to! I'm not one of your fancy men!"

"I'm not a-gonna tell you again, Bart. Get out, and don't come back."

Madden wanted to whip out his derringer and put a hole in Stone's head, but Stone would shoot him first. "You'll pay for this," he mumbled. "You're forgetting who you're dealing with."

Madden stormed past Jamie, who read the threat on his lips.

"Leave us alone," Belle said to Jamie.

The mute followed Madden out the door. Madden and Jamie glowered at each other in the corridor, then Madden turned and descended the stairs.

Jamie returned to his room, lit a cigarette, puffed nervously. Belle was disintegrating before his eyes, fear and frustration boiled inside him, couldn't let it out like normal people. He wondered what transpired between John Stone and Belle behind the closed door.

"You don't look happy to see me, Johnny."

"What's Madden doing here?"

She wrapped her arms around his waist. "You don't have anything to be jealous of. The man's nothing compared to you."

Her breath heavily scented with whiskey, eyes half-closed, unsteady on her feet, Stone led her to the sofa. "Madden's a snake in the grass."

"I don't trust nobody," she said thickly. "I don't even trust you."

"I never lied to you. I told you I was engaged."

"That din't stop you from a-crawlin' into my bed last night."

"I couldn't resist," he confessed.

She moved toward him, pressed her lips against his temple. "I'll do anything for you, Johnny."

He couldn't push her away. She licked his ear insidiously, tickles ran up his spine, he fell back to the cushions. Her hand groped for his belt buckle.

• • •

The moon rolled over a fluffy blanket of clouds. Amos Twimby climbed down from his horse, pulled the bag of gold ore from the saddle, threw it over his shoulder. Prospectors slept in their raggedy tents fifty yards away. Twenty-five thousand dollars' worth of gold ore would cause a sensation, Lodestone the topic of dinner conversation across America tomorrow.

Twimby giggled as he descended the mine. He could steal the ore and disappear, but loved to cheat and snitch, outsmart other people, make him feel he wasn't the wretched nothing he deep-down believed he was.

He wasn't strong, handsome, fast with a gun, or particularly likable, but wanted desperately to make his mark on the world. In a few days, Lodestone would overflow with new citizens, he'd gloat over his cleverness behind the scenes.

He scooped up holes in the bottom of the mine, dropped a few chunks of genuine gold ore into each, emptied the bag quickly, then climbed out of the mine and returned to his horse. *If only I could see their faces in the morning.*

"Lodestone, one hour!"

Randy LaFollette sat alone at a table, cup of coffee in front of him. A Negro porter dozed behind the bar. The rest of the parlor car was empty, other passengers asleep, the train thundered alongside a vast lake gleaming in the moonlight.

Randy LaFollette pulled down his leather satchel, removed his gunbelt, strapped it on. His choice of weapon was the Smith & Wesson Model Three, most modern up-to-date revolver made. The Board of Ordnance of the U.S. Army said it was "decidedly superior" to every other revolver tested. Not available on the open market yet, LaFollette obtained an early production model for thirty-five dollars. The ability to load and eject cartridges faster than anything else was its main innovative feature. He dropped it into his well-oiled holster.

The Negro porter behind the bar watched through sleepy eyes. "Plannin' to shoot somebody, boss?"

Randy LaFollette tied the bottom of the holster to his leg, then checked position, balance, feel. He took off his jacket, stood in the middle of the aisle, fast-drew. "That's pretty quick, boss."

Randy LaFollette whirled, drew again, spun, ducked, fanned the hammer, danced around the parlor car, killing imaginary adversaries. One moment his hand empty, the next it carried the Smith & Wesson. He pirouetted, drew again, the gun pointed between the Negro porter's eyes. "Don't worry, boy," he said to the porter nearly twice his age. "It's not loaded." LaFollette tossed a card on the bar. The porter bent over and and read the words THE UNDERTAKER.

"Can I get you another drink, boss?"

"If it's not too much trouble."

"Never too much trouble for you, Mr. LaFollette."

The gunfighter returned to his table. He retrieved a box of cartridges from his valise and loaded the Smith & Wesson. The porter poured a stiff shot of whiskey. Two days from now in Saint Louis, he'd tell his son he waited on the fastest gun alive.

"Belle, something I've got to tell you."

They lay naked in her bed, entwined in each other's arms. A candle burned on the dresser, illuminating an oil painting of naked nymphs cavorting in a meadow.

She touched her lips to his throat. "What is it, honey?"

"I told you I wasn't going to stay in town long, and . . ."

She stiffened in his arms. "You're not leavin'!"

"Noon tomorrow. Got a job with the railroad. Told you I'm headed for San Francisco. Sorry."

A sob escaped her lips. He hugged her. "Doesn't mean I don't care about you, Belle. But I belong to somebody else. I don't know how to explain it any better." He felt her tears against his cheek.

"Why don't nothin' work out for me, Johnny?"

"Doesn't work out for anybody else either."

"We got somethin' special between us, and you know it. Take me with you. I'll do anything you say."

"Can't."

She opened her mouth to plead, pride stopped her. She pushed him away, rolled over, got out of bed. "You're a son of a bitch just like the rest of them. You just got a smoother line of shit."

She pulled on her robe. He crawled out of bed and got dressed, she reached for the whiskey bottle. "Every man I ever wanted, left me," she muttered. "Every man I didn't want, can't get 'em out of my hair."

He strapped on his heavy Colts, bare-chested in the light of the candle. She watched through heavy-lidded eyes. "Don't worry about old Belle. I'll git along."

He placed his arms around her. "Maybe I'd better find a hotel room for the night."

"Like hell you will. Git downstairs and make sure my saloon's all right, if'n you want to git paid a-fore you leave. As for where you're a-gonna sleep, you can put them muddy boots under Belle McGuinness's bed any day."

She tried to tough it out, tears betrayed her. He kissed them from her cheeks. "I'm sorry," he whispered.

Gail gazed out her open window at mountaintops bathed in moonlight. The breeze fluttered diaphanous white curtains, carrying the scent of distant pine and fir forests.

She couldn't put John Stone out of her mind. Everything reminded her of him. He was like Greek sculpture in the Boston Museum. Whenever he moved, she felt strange sensations. Something magnetic in his eyes. *I think I've fallen in love with him!*

She couldn't understand it. *How can I love a man I don't even know?* She wasn't even sure what love was. Confused, bewildered, frustrated, she fidgeted beneath her blankets.

She imagined him lying naked on top of her. *I'm losing my mind.* She rolled onto her stomach and thought of him lying beneath her. Tears filled her eyes. *I can't take much more of this.*

She got out of bed, put on her robe. *What does a woman do if she wants a man? She flirts, but who wants to be a flirt? I hate flirts.*

I'll probably never see him again. Emptiness filled her heart. Knock on her door, she nearly jumped out of her slippers. Patricia said, "I heard you as I passed by. Are you all right?"

"Can't sleep."

Patricia entered the bedroom, noticed tears on Gail's cheeks. "What's wrong?"

"You'll laugh at me."

"Promise I won't." Patricia raised her right hand.

Gail covered her leaky nose with her hankie. "How can I

explain to somebody that I love him without making a fool of myself?"

"John Stone? You poor dear!" Patricia hugged her sister. "Do you think he loves you?"

"He has a fiancée in San Francisco. I don't know what to do."

"Let me tell you a story. Once, when I was about your age, I took a walk by myself in Bangor. In the park where the cannon is, I met a lumberjack. At first he frightened me, he was so big and burly, just like John Stone, but then we started talking, he was very gentle. After a half hour, if he'd crooked his finger at me, I'd follow him anywhere. But he didn't, and I married a man from a good family, with good prospects, and look how I ended up. Sometimes I wonder what would've happened if I told that lumberjack I loved him. Maybe I'd be in a broken-down little cabin in Penobscot County, washing his filthy lumberjack clothes in a tub, but I'd be a damn sight happier than I am now."

The Grand Palace Saloon was jam-packed with wall-to-wall late-night revelers, chuck-a-luck wheels spun, cards flipped over, men hollered greetings to each other from across the massive enclosed space.

On the stage, the band played a reel. Whores and miners crowded the dance floor, hopping like storks. Stone drew himself a mug of beer, sat at a table against the wall, blew out the candle.

He thought of Belle. She played him the way a violinist played her instrument. A ranch in Texas, his highest aspiration, within grasp.

If only I could do it. Impossible. Ten ranches weren't worth one Marie. *When I find her, we'll build our own ranch.*

What if I don't find her? What'm I throwing away? He felt sick in the pit of his stomach. *I've been unfaithful to Marie and I'm leaving Belle in the lurch. What kind of man am I? How'll I ever look Marie in the eye again, even if I do find her?*

"Here you are in the dark again." Edgar Faraday doffed his hat. "Moffitt told me you're the man who shot Tod Buckalew. You're a better story than the stories I sent you out on." He took out his notepad. "How'd you beat Tod Buckalew?"

Stone leaned toward him and looked into his eyes. "There never was any substantial gold in this region. Lodestone was built on one salted mine."

"Prove it."

"Marshal Kincaid's an outlaw."

"Evidence please?"

"The man who robbed me on the train had an odd-shaped scar near his eye, so does Kincaid."

"No court of law will convict on a scar. You're wasting your time. Did you talk with the three birds on top of the Sheffield yet?"

Stone related their tale of wealth and madness. Faraday wrote it swiftly on his notepad. "Now this is something that interests people, the rich man's unhappy just like the rest of us. It's horse manure, but sounds good. Maybe I can throw in some cheap philosophy." Faraday handed Stone payment for the story. "You ever need a job in the future, look me up. You're a natural-born newspaperman."

8

THE TRAIN WHISTLE blew. A single passenger stepped to the platform, valise in hand. The train conductor tipped his hat. Randy LaFollette headed toward the main street of Lodestone.

The train pulled out of the station, jets of steam roiled into scrub grass alongside the rails. LaFollette pulled his hat low over his eyes, saloons everywhere, tinkling pianos, reminded him of before he met Amanda.

A wild time in his life. One day he slept with three different women. Another five to ten years, he and Amanda could retire, live in splendor. A little Negro boy stepped out of the shadows. "Carry your bag, mister?"

"Bag's bigger than you," Randy LaFollette said. He flipped the boy a coin. "Which way's the Sheffield?"

Five hundred dollars for one fast draw and a few hours in the parlor car. Not bad at all. Randy LaFollette saw the hotel. Thick-carpeted lobby, three well-dressed gentlemen drank whiskey near the front desk. The clerk pushed the register toward him. He signed: *Joseph Smith.* A bellboy lifted the valise.

"Glad to have you with us, Mr. Smith."

Randy LaFollette followed the bellboy to the third floor. He looked out the window at a small courtyard and another tall building. The bellboy placed the valise on its stand.

"Where's the marshal's office?" asked LaFollette.

The bellboy told him, LaFollette tossed him a coin. He opened his valise, took out his work clothes. The frock coat of a suit impaired access to a man's guns.

He put on a pair of gray jeans, purple shirt, black bandanna around his neck. Then he strapped on his guns. Before the mirror, he looked at himself, a well-proportioned man, nothing special except maybe his determined cast of eye. A second later his Smith & Wesson flew into his hand, aimed at his chest. He spun around and drew again, dodged to the left, drew, wheeled, fired an imaginary shot sideways, ducked, shot another opponent, rolled to the floor, came up with the gun pointed between his eyes in the mirror.

He spun the Smith & Wesson around his finger and dropped it into its holster. Tilting his hat rakishly over his left eye, he headed for Marshal Kincaid's office.

Fully dressed, Gail stood in the dark vestibule of the Madden home, tying on her cape. Her sister fretted in the shadows. "People get killed at night. It's dangerous out there. This is a completely insane thing you're doing."

"I don't want to be like you," replied Gail, "wondering why I never followed the man I loved. I can't live with myself if I don't at least tell him."

"You'd better take this."

Gail stared at a Colt .44. "I've never fired one before."

"Just draw back the hammer with your thumb, aim, pull the trigger. The only women out this time of night are prostitutes, and men consider them fair game."

"Pray for me," Gail said.

"I should stop you. Please be careful. Don't do anything stupid."

A blue-uniformed deputy sat behind his desk, reading the *Lodestone Gazette*.

"I'm looking for Marshal Kincaid."

The deputy raised his eyes to a man of average height, made of spring steel. Hadn't heard him enter the office. "That's his door over there."

Randy LaFollette entered Kincaid's office, advanced to the desk, and stood with his legs spread slightly apart, feet rooted firmly to the floor.

"I'm here."

"Somethin' to drink?"

"Where's the money?"

Kincaid opened his desk drawer and pulled out a wad tied with a string. He threw it onto the desk. Randy LaFollette counted quickly, stuffed it into his left boot.

"What's his name?"

Gail rushed through an alley, shivering in the cool breeze. A semiconscious drunkard on the ground made a clumsy lunge for her ankle as she passed. She leapt easily over him and continued to the street, ducked into the shadows, peered around the corner of the building.

Miners staggered from saloon to saloon. Horses fretted at hitching rails. One miner punched another in the mouth, the second miner fell to the muck in the middle of the street.

The strange all-masculine world fascinated and frightened her, the worst stretch straight ahead. No point turning back now. She gripped the Colt and angled into the street.

"Hey, pretty lady," somebody called, "how's about a little?"

She made her way toward the front door of the Grand Palace. Five men stood in the middle of the street, passing a jug around. They looked like hardened rapists and murderers of the lowest sort. Taking a deep breath, she lowered her head and plowed past them.

One swung from the pack and lurched drunkenly toward her. She placed her thumb on the trigger. The miner was younger than she, with two teeth missing on top and an idiotic maniacal grin. The others turned toward her. *I should've listened to my sister.*

"Lost?" the young miner asked drunkenly. "Can I he'p you?"

"I was on my way to the Grand Palace."

"That ain't no place fer a lady. Can I take you home?"

The young miner lost his balance and fell in the mud. He struggled to get up, arms to the elbows in the smelly disgusting stuff. A gigantic miner stalked her, lifting his hat from his big pumpkin head. "I'll see you home, ma'am. That feller there cain't even stand."

"Naw, I'll look out fer the lady," insisted a miner with a

beer belly. "A decent woman wouldn't be safe with the likes of you."

"I'm going to the Grand Palace," she said. "I want to speak with John Stone."

"Last time I seen him, he was a-sittin' alone against the wall. I'll take you to him. You his wife?"

She followed beer belly into the saloon. Acrid smoke and evaporated alcohol assailed her nostrils, she coughed into her hand. Against the far wall, a line of half-naked women kicked their heels in front of a three-piece orchestra. Chuck-a-luck wheels chattered round and round, the establishment jammed with men guzzling alcoholic beverages, her eyes widened at a miner passed out on the floor. Someone emptied the vile unspeakable contents of a spittoon on him and laughed uproariously.

A man jumped on top of a bar and screamed. The bartender grabbed him by the seat of the pants and pulled him down. A miner and a whore writhed against each other in a booth, his hand up her dress.

"Here he is over here," the miner said. "Mr. Stone, yer wife's a-lookin' fer you."

Stone snapped out of his reverie and saw Gail Petigru standing in front of him. He jumped to his feet. "What're you doing here?"

"I had to talk with you."

Her face framed by the hood of her cape, she peered at his face, trying to catch a hint of his feelings. John Stone, taken by surprise, confused, complexion darkened by a blush, helped her to a chair. She pulled back the hood of her cape, the lamplight catching highlights of her lustrous black hair. She gazed at his strong cheekbones, the cleft in his chin. His intense blue eyes searched her nervously. "Are you all right?"

"I want to tell you something," she said, trying to control her quavering voice. "It's not easy for me, so I'll just come out and say it. I'm in love with you, and if you want me, we can get married. I don't know why you'd have somebody like me, but thought I'd get your reply for my diary. I make entries every day, you see. The most important things that happen to me . . ." She caught herself. *I'm prattling like an idiot.*

Glad I stopped drinking, Stone thought. He stared at the innocent young maiden and wanted to shield her from the cruelty and ugliness of the world. "If I weren't engaged to another woman, I'd marry you tomorrow."

The crowd applauded, as a man with a guitar sat on a stool in the middle of the stage. He wore the wide flaring pants of an Argentine gaucho, black hair parted on the side and slicked down, a cigarette dangled from the corner of his mouth. He strummed the guitar and sang a Spanish song in a strong baritone voice.

They saw the sun rise over the pampas, señoritas with roses in their hair. His voice carried the passion and romance of the Argentine cowboy, the love he bore for his wild freewheeling life. Few patrons spoke Spanish, but they knew what he meant.

Gail wanted to bend forward and kiss John Stone. She closed her eyes, his skin fragrant and warm against her lips. He turned to her in surprise.

"Just wanted a little one," she said, "to remember you by. Now I won't have to spend the rest of my life wondering what might've been. I hope you're not mad at me for trying." *You're babbling again.*

He reached into his shirt pocket and took out the topaz heart. "I believe this is yours."

She stared at the jewelry. "Where'd you get it?"

He shrugged mysteriously. "It's late. I'll see you home."

"I came here under my own steam, I'll leave the same way."

"I don't think you understand how dangerous it is out there."

"That's what people say, but everyone I've met so far has been a perfect gentleman. I think the hazards of Lodestone've been greatly exaggerated." She pulled the gun. "Besides, I'm not as helpless as you think."

A bartender in a dirty apron approached the table. "We're runnin' out of beer. Can you git us another keg?"

"I'll be right back," Stone said to Gail. "Wait for me."

Randy LaFollette saw the sign: GRAND PALACE.

His gait steady, primed to kill, all thoughts banished from his mind, he climbed the stairs, entered the crowded noisy saloon, headed toward the nearest bar, raised his hand. The bartender scurried toward him, wiping his hands on his apron.

"I'm looking for John Stone."

"Last time I seen him, he was over there."

Randy LaFollette turned toward a table in the darkness, perceived the dim outline of someone sitting there. He crossed the floor, shoulders squared, ready to draw and fire. To his surprise, a young woman sat at the table, eyes glued to the wailing gaucho on the stage. She turned to LaFollette as he drew closer.

"I'm looking for John Stone," he said.

"There he is over there."

A tall brawny man carried a keg of beer on his shoulder. LaFollette angled to cut him off. He leaned against a wall and waited for the big man to draw closer, noticed the old battered Confederate cavalry hat, broad expanse of chest, pants tucked into his boots, cavalry style. Hard to miss a target like that. LaFollette stuck out his foot.

Stone's ankle collided with LaFollette's boot, lost his balance, managed to push the keg away before he and it struck the floor. The keg cracked and splattered beer over everybody in the vicinity. Stone rolled, on his feet again, facing the man who'd tripped him.

LaFollette stood with his thumbs hooked in his belt. "Watch where you're going."

Stone's new clothes drenched with beer, licked some off his upper lip, wanted to punch the stranger, but the saloon manager doesn't fight with customers if he can avoid it. "Sorry."

Stone placed his hat on his head and turned away. Two bartenders arrived with mops. Randy LaFollette grabbed Stone's shoulder and spun him around. "I think you're a stupid son of a bitch!"

"It was an accident. Let me buy you a drink."

"I don't want your cheap rotgut whiskey. Where'd you get that hat? I think Bobby Lee was a stupid son of a bitch too."

The man didn't appear drunk, but maybe crazy like the one who jumped on the bar earlier. "Mister, I think you'd better go home and sleep it off."

"I just called Bobby Lee a piece of shit coward."

Stone wondered what was bothering the man. A crowd

assembled in the vicinity. Whores on the second floor lined up behind the banister and watched the confrontation, Slipchuck among them, broom in hand. John Stone faced off with a man who looked vaguely familiar.

A voice in the crowd said, "I think that's Randy LaFollette."

Excitement rippled through the saloon. Nearly everybody heard of the famous gunfighter. Slipchuck recalled his face. He'd seen him shoot somebody once in a New Mexico Comanchero town.

Stone recalled saloon conversations he'd heard about Randy LaFollette. They called him The Undertaker. Stone felt warm, his furnace turning up the heat perhaps for the last time. The devil leaned toward him and whispered: "This is your chance to find out how fast you really are."

LaFollette felt no elation at the fascination he evoked. All business, get the assignment over with. "What do I have to do to make you fight, you goddamned rebel coward?"

I don't have a prayer against him, Stone thought. *But can't turn around and walk away.* "Mr. LaFollette, I don't know you and you don't know me. What's this about?"

Randy LaFollette took a step forward and spat contemptuously in Stone's face. Stone wiped his mouth with the back of his sleeve. No one ever spit on him before, he thought his head would explode.

"They say Bobby Lee liked to sleep with little boys," sneered Randy LaFollette.

That old wild combat feeling struck John Stone. *I think I can take him.* Spit stung his face like corrosive acid. "Let's go outside."

"Looking for a chance to run away, Johnny Reb?"

"I don't run from scum."

Deathly silent in the saloon, Stone stared into Randy LaFollette's eyes. *They said Tod Buckalew was fast too, and I shot him. Dave Quarternight couldn't be beat, but I beat him. Let one man spit on you, everybody'll spit on you. You've got to draw the line someplace.*

Slipchuck broke through the crowd. "Johnny, you don't know who this man is!"

"Yes I do." Stone turned to LaFollette. "Shall we go outside?"

The crowd headed toward the doors, Gail Petigru among

them, trying to understand what was happening. *Preposterous, barbaric, a nightmare of incalculable proportions, I'll awake in bed and everything'll be all right.*

Men burst through the doors and spilled into the street. Belle heard the commotion and ran down the stairs. "What is it?" she asked one of her girls.

"Randy LaFollette just called John Stone out."

Belle slept with Randy LaFollette once long ago in a Memphis whorehouse. She pushed men out of her way as she ran across the saloon. *I've got to stop them!*

John Stone looked up at the sky. Something told him it might be the last he ever saw. At West Point they drummed it into his head every waking hour of the day: Cowardice was worse than death.

Randy LaFollette savored the moment. The whole town present, even a bunch of swells wearing evening clothes, best advertising in the world for The Undertaker. His right hand rose slowly, fingers unlimbered, legs spread apart. "Make your move."

"That's enough!" screamed Belle, breaking through the crowd. She fought her way forward and ran between them. "Stop it!"

"Hiding behind a lady's skirt, Mr. Stone?"

"Step back, Belle," Stone said. "This is none of your business."

"He'll kill you, Johnny! You don't have a chance! That there's Randy LaFollette! He's the fastest gun alive!"

"Somebody get her out of the way," replied John Stone, "before she gets shot."

Four miners detached themselves from the ground, grabbed Belle, dragged her back as she tried to bite and kick them. "Let me go! It's goddamned *murder*!"

Down the street, Marshal Kincaid sat on a second-floor balcony, boots resting on the rail, puffing his corncob. Ready to draw and fire, he had no doubts about the outcome. His John Stone problem would be over in a minute.

Stone and LaFollette measured each other in the middle of the street. Gail watched from the sidewalk, quivering with amazement and horror. Lumberjacks brawled in the barrooms of Bangor, but nothing like this.

"I'll let you go first, Johnny Reb," LaFollette said. "Whenever you're ready."

Stone grit his teeth and dived his hand toward his Colt. LaFollette saw the crease on Stone's shoulder, drew his Smith & Wesson, took aim at the massive target, pulled the trigger. A hair before tripping his hammer, Randy LaFollette was struck in the chest by a raging churning cyclone, coughed, his gun fired, the bullet flew over Stone's head.

John Stone couldn't believe he was still there. *Almost got me.* He broke out into a cold sweat. LaFollette staggered to the side, blinded by confusion and pain. He tried to raise his technologically advanced Smith & Wesson, it weighed a ton. *How could I lose?* His legs gave out and he dropped to his knees. The crowd stared at the widening dark blotch on his purple shirt. Randy LaFollette's head hung down, blood flowed out his ears, nose, and mouth. He appeared to be bowing before John Stone, as if relinquishing something.

The fastest gun alive fell on his face. All eyes turned to John Stone. Mystified, shaken, but victorious nonetheless, he dropped his gun into his holster.

Belle's skirts dragged in the mud. "How in hell you do that?"

The crowd gathered around. Mr. Moffitt slapped John Stone on the back. "Good show!"

Gail was paralyzed. A dead man lay in the street, and John Stone shot him before her very eyes! A hand dropped onto her shoulder, she nearly jumped out of her skin. "You all right, Missy?" Slipchuck asked, an expression of concern on his weather-beaten features. "Can I take you home? I won't try nothin' fancy. You don't have to worry none 'bout old Slipchuck."

She didn't feel very steady. "All right."

They walked away from the crowd swirling about John Stone. Edgar Faraday, notepad in hand, advanced toward the man who shot Randy LaFollette. "Tell me what you thought when you pulled the trigger?"

Stone felt the world out of kilter. He should be bleeding in the mud right now. *Every crazy son of a bitch in the world will try to kill me, to make their reputations.* Belle took his arm and led him toward the door. "You'd better lie down, honey. You had a hard night."

• • •

A group of uniformed deputies sat around the stove in the main room of the marshal's office.

"Unbelievable," one of them said.

"Maybe Randy LaFollette wasn't fast as everybody thought."

"He looked plenty fast to me. But John Stone was faster."

They knew the threat John Stone posed. The doorknob turned, Kincaid entered the office, lips set in a grim line. He sauntered toward the table and didn't bother sitting. "Time to move on, boys. John Stone's a-gonna be on us like stink on shit."

"There's eight of us and only one of him," Corbelli replied. "Let 'im come."

"Every lawman and soldier in the territory'll be here once John Stone starts talkin'. We best clear the hell out. He's prob'ly wirin' Fort Logan right now."

John Stone lay in the middle of Belle's bed, arms and legs flung out, eyes closed, alone, all lights extinguished. He tried to calm down. For a moment he'd seen the bowels of hell in Randy LaFollette's gun. When his Colt fired, he thought it was LaFollette's Smith & Wesson. He even felt something strike his heart, but the famous gunfighter rocked back on his heels. *I don't know how I beat him, but I did. Maybe I'm the fastest gun alive.*

That's the most dangerous thought you can have. Forget about it. But he couldn't. Was he unbeatable? Could he walk through the world like a god, because no one could kill him?

He almost beat me. I could be a corpse right now. He felt exhausted. His heart and brain slowed after an unusually long and stressful day. He went slack on the bed, listening to cannons fire at Bloody Sharpsburg.

Two figures passed through a dark alley littered with garbage. A rat lurking beside a trash barrel watched them pass, twitching his nose. A bad smell came from them.

Jamie carried a tin of coal oil in each hand, Belle dressed like a man in a long coat and cowboy hat. They crossed the street, entered another alley, Jamie muttering and mumbling below his breath, trying to change her mind, she paid no attention to him.

She intended to kill Rebecca Hawkins, nothing would stop her now. The preacher woman went too far. Men killed each other for far less, humiliation kept returning, alternating with fierce hatred for its perpetrator. Dried-out bitch. *I'll teach her to point her finger at me.*

They came to the preacher lady's house, surrounded by a fence. Dead flowers bordered the front porch. Belle nodded to Jamie. He made a griping sound, she responded with a mean face. They glanced around the quiet neighborhood, all lights out. Each took a tin of coal oil and poured it around the wooden base of the house. The night air filled with powerful chemical fumes.

Coal oil splashed onto her boots as she walked along the wall. Belle didn't falter once. Burn her like bacon in the fire. Jamie appeared around the far end of the house. They moved toward each other, poured final drops of coal oil onto rags they brought with them.

Jamie flicked a match and lit the coal oil at the base of the house. It caught flame and crept slowly around the unpainted wooden shakes. Belle held oil-soaked rags in her hand, Jamie lit them with a match. Belle tossed fire through an open window. They watched tongues of flame creep up the walls of the preacher lady's house.

Rebecca Hawkins, naked but for her nail-studded leather belt, knelt on the floor of her room, delirious from lack of food and sleep, her waist a band of festering suppurating pain.

She passed in and out of consciousness. *Why have you abandoned me, my Lord?* She saw a grotesque monster eating the infant Jesus. *Never felt so spiritually bereft, what if it's all a fairy tale?*

A sob escaped her throat. She felt worthless, hopeless, lost. She'd done all the right things in her life. Every day she prayed for at least two hours, fasted every sabbath, mortified her flesh, denied herself the decent wholesome pleasures of home and hearth in the unceasing pursuit of God's love. *Give me a sign. Otherwise I have no reason to give.*

A ribbon of flame danced in front of her. *There it is!* She reached toward it, her fingertips burned. *I dwell within unapproachable fire.* She bowed her head and clasped her hands together. "My God," she uttered, "you've shown yourself glorious to me." Elated, she burst into tears of joy. Dancing flames encircled her, something crashed, sparks sprayed into the air. She coughed, floor hot, tiny whirls of smoke creeping through cracks between boards. *I'm coming, Lord.*

A lick of flame seared her cheek. Another set fire to her hair. Pain needles dug into her skull. She leapt to her feet and screamed, "This is hell!" Sheets of flame ran up the walls, her eyebrows scorched, air torrid in her lungs as she tried to breathe. She staggered from side to side. A glimmer of something terrible came to her mind. *Judge not that ye be not judged, for as ye judge, so shall ye be judged.* Smoke and heat overcame the preacher lady, she fell to the floor, her skin crackled and spattered, she'd never point that finger again.

Belle and Jamie ran across a deserted street. Behind them, fire reached toward the heavens. They darted into an alley and passed a miner lying on his stomach, a knife protruding out the middle of his back.

Hoofbeats in the street, they pressed their backs to the wall of the alley. Wagons and men on horseback roared past, heading toward the northern part of town. Belle and Jamie waited until they passed, then ran across the intersection, paused to catch their breaths in the shadows on the far side of the street. *Whoever they are, they're in an awful hurry,* Belle thought. The sky was bright at the east end of town. "Fire!" A bell clanged.

She and Jamie slunk through the shadows, heading for the back door of the Grand Palace.

Kincaid rode at the head of the wagons and men on horseback galloping away from Lodestone. He heard the fire bell and turned around to look at the town where he'd enjoyed the greatest success of his life. *Hope the whole damn place burns down, with John Stone in it.*

Hard to believe John Stone outdrew Randy LaFollette, but saw it with my own eyes. Maybe John Stone's Jesse James. His wife held the reins of two horses pulling the wagon, money and valuables stored in crates, other supplies at the hideout, ten members of the gang lived there permanently.

Had to end someday, Kincaid thought. He wondered if the cavalry would come after them. No fun to go on the dodge at his age, with a nagging wife. That goddamned John Stone. *Of all the trains in Colorado, why'd I have to rob his?*

Belle looked out the window of her bedroom, a patch of sky orange on the far side of town. She heard something click behind her. "Don't move," said John Stone from the bed.

"It's me."

Stone thought somebody had come to kill him. He holstered his guns. "What's out the window?"

"A fire."

He came behind her, placed his hands on her hips. "Where've you been?"

"In my office downstairs."

"I'd better check the saloon."

"The bartenders know what to do, and if they don't, I'll fire 'em. Meanwhile, I need a bath."

She sat on a chair and pulled off her boots. A strange odor filled the room. She walked in stocking feet to the maid's quarters. Stone lifted one of her boots. How'd she spill coal oil in her office?

9

UPON ARRIVING AT the bank next morning, Bart Madden learned the incredible news. John Stone outgunned Randy LaFollette. Marshal Kincaid and his law deputies left town, under suspicion of robbery. *What if John Stone finds out I put up half the money to hire Randy LaFollette?*

Bart Madden feared John Stone. The man who shot Randy LaFollette was no one to trifle with. The town in an uproar, he worried about a run on the bank. With no marshal, depositors wanted to safeguard their money.

He reached to an inside pocket and pulled out his derringer. *Maybe I should blow my brains out and get it over with.* He held the gun to his head. Swallowing hard, he returned the derringer to his pocket.

They'll lynch me if the bank runs out of money. How'd I get into this mess? He wished Belle were there to comfort him, but she lay in bed with John Stone. Wherever he looked, the source of his trouble was John Stone.

Once word got out that Lodestone was wide open, outlaws would descend like buzzards on a dead cow. *First place they'll come is the bank. But the crowd'll clean me out first. I'm finished.*

He sat at his desk and buried his face in his hands. How'd it happen? He planned everything cleverly, nothing left to chance. Then he got mixed up with Belle. She derailed him more than anything.

He thought of her lying naked in bed, except for her diamond necklace. How wonderful to make love with a drunken woman, nothing she wouldn't do. Dumped him like an old tattered dishrag after John Stone showed up.

Arrogant son of a bitch. Walks around like he's still in the Reb army. Who the hell does he think he is? More'n one way to kill a man.

His chief teller appeared in the doorway, anxiety etched into his face. "Sir, time to open the doors."

Madden glanced at his watch. Nine o'clock on the dot. "Go ahead, Sutherland."

Pale as mountain snow, the chief teller walked down the corridor to the front door. The two other tellers examined his face for guidance in the looming disaster. At least a hundred men waited in the street to withdraw their money. The head teller opened the doors.

The men lined up, the first bank book thrown down.

"Wanna git all me money."

Madden lit a cheroot. *They might even tar and feather me when the money runs out. Maybe I'll be hung from the nearest tree. Should I get out of town right now, while I have the chance?*

Dr. White opened the door of his office and saw John Stone standing in front of him, crisscrossed gunbelts and enormous shoulders. Stone removed his old Confederate cavalry hat. "I'd like to see the deceased."

The coroner led Stone to a small room at the back of his house. Randy LaFollette lay stretched out naked on a table, ugly mangled purple crater in the middle of his chest. His complexion pale blue, eyes closed, mouth at peace, the fastest gun alive dead as a mackerel.

"He had this card in his wallet," Dr. White said.

IN CASE OF ACCIDENT OR DEATH
NOTIFY AMANDA LAFOLLETTE
CRESCENT HOTEL, DENVER

"I understand he had a large sum of money on him," Stone said.

"Oh, yes, of course. I forgot all about it. Ha ha. I'll get it."

Randy LaFollette commanded a high price for his skills. Stone figured he was carrying the money with him, and if anybody was entitled to it, it was him.

The doctor returned with the wad of bills. "Might as well turn it over to you," he said nervously. "Wondered who to give it to. Wasn't gonna keep it for myself, you understand."

Stone flipped through the sheaf of paper money. Five hundred dollars.

"What's going on out there?" asked the doctor.

Stone looked out the window. Men danced and screamed in the middle of the street. "Gold! We hit the mother lode!"

The owners of the Western Sovereign Mine held burlap bags full of ore. The magic word passed from lip to ear like a disease. *Gold!*

The crowd grew as news spread like wildfire across Lodestone. A box was brought forward, the president of the Western Sovereign Mine stepped upon it. Twenty-five years old, wearing a floppy-brimmed hat, already seriously inebriated, he reached into his burlap bag and came out with a lump of ore, held it in the air, tried to speak. The crowd roared.

He blithered, appeared insane. "I was asleep, and a voice said: *Albert, go down in that mine, you'll find gold.* I thought it was just another crazy dream, but then I thought *what the hell.* So I put on my clothes and went to the mine, crawled down into it, lit me lantern. Then I started digging. I only went down a little ways when I found this!" He held up a lump of ore. "We hit the mother lode!"

The crowd dispersed to get their picks and shovels. The officers of the Western Sovereign Mine headed toward the Lodestone Savings Bank, to deposit their great wealth in the safe. Everyone made way for the heroes. They reached the tellers' cage, placed their bags on the counter.

"Want to put this in our account."

Miners lined up to return funds just withdrawn. In his private office, Bart Madden drank a sip of brandy. He'd forgotten the salted mine, but the same trick worked again. Goddamn idiots didn't suspect anything. A knock on his door.

"Come in."

Jonas Brodbent approached his desk, a conspiratorial grin on his face. Somebody fired a gun in the street. "Gold!"

someone shouted. "They found gold!"

Madden and Brodbent shook hands. "You saved my life," Madden said. "I'll never forget you."

Unable to restrain their glee, they embraced and danced a jig in the middle of the floor.

Stone sat on a chair in Belle's living room and stuffed his belongings into his saddlebags. He didn't know whether to go after Kincaid, or continue to San Francisco.

I can't let Kincaid get away with it. Have to look over my shoulder for him the rest of my life. The train's leaving for San Francisco in two hours. What should I do?

Slipchuck entered the living room, a glum expression on his face. "Cain't leave. This whorehouse is in me blood. I know we're pards and all, but this is the best job I ever had."

"You said you wanted to go to San Francisco, the only place you never been. You're giving that up to push a broom in a whorehouse?"

Slipchuck placed his hand on Stone's shoulder and said solemnly, "I'd give my left ball to push a broom in this whorehouse."

Belle carried a tray covered with eggs, bacon, home fried potatoes, loaf of bread, pot of blueberry jam. Washed, coiffed, cosmetics carefully applied, she wore a blue and white polka dot silk robe.

"Made up yer mind?" she asked Stone. She passed him a plate covered with food.

Slipchuck said, "You can't take on Kincaid and his gang alone, Johnny. Too many of 'em."

"You never know when you might run into Kincaid again," said Belle. "He tried to kill you the nice way, but it din't work. Next time he might bushwhack you."

Turmoil and disturbance in the vestibule, then the mayor, president of the town council, numerous politicians and business leaders, plus Mr. Moffitt of the Kansas Pacific Railroad, entered the living room.

"We'd like to have a word with John Stone," the mayor said in his stentorian voice. Stone arose from his chair. The mayor shook his hand. "Congratulations on your fine display of shooting. We've just had an emergency meeting, decided to offer you the post of marshal, salary one hundred dollars per month."

"Who's Mr. Moffitt?" asked Belle.

Everyone turned to her, resplendent in her tight-fitting silk robe, a cigar held between her fingers. The railroad magnate stepped forward and bowed. "I am at your service, madam."

She held out her dovelike hand. He took it and touched his lips to the tips of her fingers, then raised his head and took a step back, slurping up her magnificent figure with his eyes.

"I was a-thinkin'," Belle said, "that the railroad should put up some money for a posse, since Kincaid and his boys've robbed so many trains. The rest of us business people should kick in too. We let Kincaid run loose, no tellin' what he might do."

Moffitt's eyes were affixed to her breasts. They were round, firm, upstanding, perfectly shaped, he imagined the pert nipple in his mouth. His eyes touched hers, he felt a mad vibration deep at the base of his spine.

Stone watched Belle work her feminine wiles on the railroad tycoon's mind. Spots of emotion appeared on Moffitt's cheeks as he cleared his throat and said, "I pledge one thousand dollars to the men who bring in Bill Kincaid, dead or alive."

Amanda woke late that morning. She reached beside her for Randy, but he was gone. Opening her eyes, she remembered his assignment. But he always came back.

She performed her morning toilet, thinking of the odd turns a life can take. How could anyone guess she'd marry a gunfighter? Occasionally she read a story in an out-of-town newspaper about the notorious Randy LaFollette shooting someone. Difficult to connect the gunfighter with her loving and considerate husband.

She was spoiled, he always deferred to her, did anything she asked, loved her with complete devotion. He was all she ever wanted. She couldn't imagine her gentleman killing anybody.

She descended the stairs to the lobby. "Mrs. LaFollette?"

She turned to the front desk. "Yes?"

"Telegram for you."

He always wired to say he loved her, advised of his return. Eagerly she swept toward the desk, plucked the telegram from the clerk's hands. Long fingernails impatiently tore a paper seam, she pulled out the document and unfolded it.

RANDY LAFOLLETTE SHOT LAST NIGHT IN LODESTONE
PLEASE ADVISE.

MARSHAL JOHN STONE

Kincaid looked at cracks in the walls of his log cabin. The ceiling leaked, floor crooked, two windows wouldn't open. He pounded his fist on the table. "Goddamned John Stone!"

His wife threw a length of wood into the cookstove. Born and raised in a shack like this, she could handle it. She jabbed the antelope steak with a fork, dropped it onto a plate, laid it before her husband.

"I hope you're not plannin' to send the wimmin' away, Bill. We won't stand for it, if'n you try."

"Then you'll sit fer it or lay fer it, but you're all leavin', and don't gimme no guff. The army'll find us any day. We cain't fight with wimmin here."

"We'll take care of ourselves. Just give us rifles."

He grabbed her forearm. "You don't git it, so I'll tell you again. I don't want you to git shot before my eyes. I might be strong, but not that strong. If you don't leave on yer own steam, I'll cold-conk you, tie you to the back of a horse, boot his ass on out of here."

Edgar Faraday entered Bart Madden's office. "You wanted to see me?"

"What're you writing about the Western Sovereign?"

"Most promising strike since the Comstock."

Madden smiled. "I can see you know your business. You're getting out a special edition?"

"Special editions are expensive . . ."

"Send me the bill. Mail copies to every major newspaper in America. Let's pump this up as much as we can."

"Postage is expensive these days."

"I'll pay for everything. And you don't have to mention the shooting last night, or the house that burned down. We all know what happened. A waste of valuable space that could be devoted to our school system, fire department, scenic beauties, ideal climate, you know what I mean, but the main story is the hills're full of gold, just like the last time we did this, remember?"

"I never fully appreciated the power of the press before I met you, Mr. Madden."

Belle gazed at her reflection in the mirror, light from windows illuminating her features. Still beautiful as ever, she thought happily, applying soft pats of rouge to her cheeks. *Maybe I can convince John Stone to stay forever*. She took another drink of whiskey. *I'll love him so much he won't have time to think of anybody else. He needs somebody to take care of him.*

Something moved behind her. The preacher lady, in her high-necked black dress, undulated in the afternoon sunlight. "Murderess, spawn of the devil, do you think you've escaped the judgment of God?" She pointed her long accusing finger at Belle. "The Lord God sees everything! You'll burn in the fires of hell!"

Belle threw a bottle of perfume at the apparition, screamed hysterically, lunged for her throat, but the preacher lady dissolved, Belle crashed into the wall.

She cowered beside a chair and searched the bedroom. *Maybe I should knock off the booze.*

John Stone wore a tin badge on his fringed buckskin jacket, stood with Slipchuck before a map of the territory that showed caves and out-of-the-way canyons where an outlaw gang could hide.

"Won't be easy to pick up their trail," Slipchuck said. "Too many horses comin' in and out of town from all directions. The onliest thing to do is work in circles and hope we cut their tracks." Slipchuck spat a gob of brown tobacco juice into the cuspidor. "Them outlaws won't hang around long. Split up and meet someplace else a month or two down the line."

Little Annie Mae, the dancer from the Grand Palace, slipped into the marshal's office. She wore no makeup and looked like an eight-year-old street urchin, eyes red from crying. "Can I talk to you alone?" she asked John Stone.

He led her to his office. She dropped to a chair in front of his desk, unbuttoning her voluminous brown wool coat.

"You done me a favor onc't," she said. "I figger I owes you one." She fidgeted in her chair. He waited for her to speak. She was like a child afraid of being scolded. "I had me a boyfriend a while back," she said in a little voice, "one of Kincaid's deputies. I went out to see 'im a few times at the hideout. I can tell you whar it is."

Madden made his way to the living room of his house. His wife and sister-in-law sat crocheting, rifles leaning against their chairs. "Look who's home," Patricia said sarcastically. "My lord and protector. If we had to rely on you, we'd be in trouble."

"You're in no danger. We've got a new marshal, our erstwhile supper guest John Stone. May I speak with you alone, Patricia?"

"If you have anything to say to me, say it in front of my sister. She knows everything anyway. Do you think she doesn't have ears?"

"She can have feathers for all I care." A bad marriage burst out his throat. "I'm leaving you. Hereafter, we'll communicate through our lawyers. The only reason I'm not throwing you out of this house is I don't want a scandal. I'm sick of you, and hope I never see you again."

Patricia burst into tears. Bart strolled proudly to the stairs. Free of the bitch at last.

The posse gathered in front of the marshal's office, waiting for John Stone to lead them to the outlaw hideout. Nearby, a wagon was loaded with extra ammunition, supplies, and tents. Men checked and rechecked their equipment. "When the hell we leavin'?" one grumbled. "Din't jine the posse to stand in the middle of the street all damn day."

"I knows why you joined, Tab." The miner rubbed his thumb and fingers together. "Fer the dinero like the rest of us."

Madden, carrying his valise on his shoulder, advanced down the middle of the street. "When're you boys going after Kincaid?"

"Soon as John Stone gets up off his ass and takes charge."

"It's a wild goose chase, you ask me. There's a lot of country out there. Be like finding a needle in a haystack."

"Not anymore," a man in a brown derby said. "We know where Kincaid's holed up. Somebody blabbered."

Madden's good humor turned sour and rancid. Instead of continuing to the Sheffield Hotel, he raced toward the building where Brodbent maintained his office. He climbed the stairs and entered the assayer's office without knocking. Brodbent looked up from a lump of ore from the salted Western Sovereign Mine. "A trainload of prospectors is on their way from Kansas City. Better buy a bigger safe for your bank, Madden. You'll need it."

"We've got to warn Kincaid about the posse."

Brodbent pshawed. "Don't worry about the posse. They'll never find Kincaid."

"They know where the hideout is, you fool. Somebody talked. You'd better send a rider to warn Kincaid."

The full implications struck Brodbent. He ran out the office, down the stairs, across the street, sped through an alley, jumped over a pile of drunks, crossed a backyard.

Twimby lived in a tiny room furnished with bed, small table, and chair on the second floor of a dilapidated old building at the edge of Niggertown. The corner of a magazine poked out from underneath the pillow. Brodbent pulled it free and looked at the cover, a drawing of two naked women lying in bed. Flipping through the pages, he saw more nude women performing a variety of lewd acts.

Twimby shifted his feet nervously. "Feller give me that. Din't buy it meself."

Brodbent threw the magazine on the bed. "Get a fast horse, tell Kincaid that Stone knows where the hideout is, and he'd better move out fast!"

Twimby ran down the stairs. Brodbent heard the front door of the building slam. He waited a few moments, then picked up the girlie magazine, tucked it into his shirt, headed back to his office, where he could examine the artwork in solitude.

Posse members smoked cigarettes, drank whiskey, fussed with guns. The street filled with people, excitement ran high, incredible events in their little town.

"Let's git started!" somebody shouted.

Another posse member, too many tokes from his flask, yanked out his gun and fired at the sky. Children jumped with glee and clapped their hands. Women watched apprehensively; posses often left widows with hungry mouths to feed.

Stone stepped onto the planked sidewalk, a ray of sun caught his bright new badge, his old Confederate cavalry hat low over his eyes. He was followed by Slipchuck, the mayor, several politicians, and Tobias Moffitt, thumbs hooked in his suspenders. Stone stood before the posse like an ex-cavalry officer addressing his troopers. "If there's anybody with doubts, this is the time to step back! We can expect Kincaid and his men to put up a tough fight! You think this is a turkey roast, stay home!"

Not a man budged, not even those with doubts. Others hoped there'd be fighting, booty, high adventure, something to brag about next time they went to a saloon.

"A fighting force can't be effective," Stone continued, "unless there's *one* leader! When I tell you to do something, I expect you to get it done."

They remembered Stone's gun duel with Randy LaFollette. No one wanted to challenge him. Stone and Slipchuck untied their horses' reins from the hitching post, climbed into saddles, Stone pulled the reins of his chestnut roan gelding to the left. He'd never ridden the animal before, but Slipchuck, first-class judge of horseflesh, picked it out for him.

The chestnut roan broke into a gallop. From the top floor of the Grand Palace, Belle McGuinness watched John Stone lead the posse in a thunder of hooves down the middle of the street.

Slipchuck trotted beside him, wiry and agile in his saddle, and then came the twenty-odd posse members. One leaned his head back and skillfully dripped whiskey from his flask into his mouth.

Belle watched the posse turn the corner. Stone passed from her sight, followed by his men. She slammed the window closed. On the dresser sat a bottle half full of whiskey. She pulled the plug and took a swig.

Opposite her, on the wall, hung a gaudy oil painting of Saint Sebastian, his naked body pierced with countless arrows. She worried about John Stone. *I instigated him to go after Kincaid. If Johnny gets hit by a stray bullet, be my fault.*

She bit her thumbnail anxiously. *He'll leave me anyway, don't care about me at all.* She took another swallow of *whiskey. I was just another good hot whore to pass the time until he can marry his lady love.*

Something caught her eye. A pale indistinct figure in a black dress stood against the drapes. "You'd sacrifice the man you love to satiate your disgusting passions! You're capable of any foul deed! Nothing is sacred to you! When will you open your eyes to the truth of Christ!" The preacher lady pointed her long bony finger at her. "You'll never escape me! No matter where you are, I'll be there! I won't let you sleep until you bow your head and repent to the Lord God!"

"Repent for what?" Belle screamed. She picked up a small statuette of a Greek Olympic athlete and hurled it. The granite figure crashed against heavy drapes and fell to the floor. The preacher lady vanished.

Madden paced back and forth in his office. He couldn't sit down. His mouth tasted like a dead clam from smoking cheroot after cheroot. Turbulent thoughts flooded his mind like a river overflowing its banks. His wife dismissed from his mind, he concentrated his obsessive nature on Belle.

She threw me out like I was an old shoe. Cut off my balls and I let her get away with it. He pounded his fist on a file cabinet. *She's just a blowsy whiskey-smelling slut from the cribs, how dare she treat me that way after all I did for her?* Outraged indignation surged through him. He pinched his lips together. *What can I do?*

He collapsed on the chair behind his desk. Women, god-damn them. *Not her insults that bother me most,* he admitted ruefully. *I love her, but she tossed me out.* He lit another cheroot, remembered tumbling in bed with that magnificent body, soft and firm at the same time, milk a man dry. A few times he left her bedroom so weak he could barely walk.

No one else ever did that for him. It was like a drug. He had to have her. She couldn't deny his need. Horrible to think of her doing the same wonderful things to John Stone. He imagined them in bed together, something snapped in his mind.

Got to try one last time. She won't take me back, I'll kill the bitch before I let her sleep with another man.

Twimby, secret admirer of naked women, rode low in his saddle, wind whistling through his beard, eyes glittering with delight as he searched for the gorge straight ahead.

He knew every shortcut, switchback, and runaround in the territory, couldn't wait to see the expression on Kincaid's face when he made his report. He whipped the reins on the horse's flanks. A gob of saliva flew from the animal's mouth into the air. Twimby saw something move behind the tree trunks on both sides of the trail. He dug his spurs into the horse's flanks and lay his cheek against the animal's massive curving neck. "Yoowieee!"

The injuns pulled back their bowstrings and shot a hail of arrows. One whacked his leg. Twimby nearly jumped out of his saddle, blacked out momentarily from the pain, arrows flew like hornets, then he was out of range, horse speeding onward. Twimby reached down, broke off the end of the arrow before it snagged something. Tossing the feathers and shaft over his shoulder, his right leg a solid column of pain, he continued grimly on his mission to warn Kincaid.

Jamie Boggs walked down the third-floor corridor, heading toward his office at the head of the stairs. The maid told him Belle was drinking heavily and talking to the walls. His brow furrowed with worry, he couldn't hear the creak of a floorboard behind him. A Colt slammed against his head. His eyes rolled up and he crashed to the floor. Bart Madden stood over him, gun in hand. He smacked Boggs again, to make sure he wouldn't get up soon. Then he dragged the slack body into the dark shadows off the main corridor. Blood oozed from a dent in Jamie's skull and trickled down his cheek.

Madden was hatless, hair mussed, a weird gleam in his eyes. Events of the past day knocked him loose from conventional patterns of behavior. Belle's abrupt dismissal of him rankled deeply. Maybe she'd listen to reason now that Stone was out of sight. Silently he opened the door to her apartment and slunk inside. The living room was empty. He continued to the bedroom and found her sleeping in a pale pink chemise.

His movement stirred her. "What the hell're *you* doing here?"

He looked crazed, demonic, gun in hand. "You're forgetting the good times we had," he said excitedly. "You can't just throw it all away. Now let's have a talk, Belle. I told you I'd marry you. A man can't give a woman more than that."

The gun in his hand didn't intimidate her. "Now you listen to me. Marriage was what I wanted more'n anything else, but you wouldn't have me because I wasn't respectable enough. Then John Stone came along. What was I supposed to do, look the other way? By the Jesus, he's gorgeous. Yes, I love him, I'm not ashamed to say it. You an' me're finished."

He grinned arrogantly. "Where'll you go after Kincaid kills your great John Stone?"

"They'll never see each other. Johnny'll be back in a few days. That posse ain't nothin' more'n a riding exhibition."

Madden narrowed his eyes triumphantly. "You're misinformed, by dear. John Stone knows exactly where the hideout is, but Kincaid's been warned. He'll bushwhack that bunch of drunks, crazy old men, and saddle tramps. Then you'll come crawling back to me, and maybe I'll forgive you, who knows?"

Belle stared at him in disbelief. *I've got to warn Johhny.* "Get out of my bedroom. I'm changin' clothes."

"You've forgotten the things we said to each other in that bed over there. Didn't they mean anything to you?"

"I say 'em to all my customers, and that's all you was after you said you wasn't a-gonna marry me. I wasn't good enough for you, eh? Well, now you're not good enough for me. I'll change clothes in front of you if you won't git the hell out. I don't give a goddamn either way!"

She pulled her man's pants and shirt out of the closet, then took off her chemise. He gazed at her beautiful naked body, lust overwhelmed him, he clasped her in his arms. "You can't do this to me!"

She squirmed and tried to break away. He held her tighter and pressed his lips against her cheek. Quick as a minx, she dug her teeth into his lip. Blood spurted against his tongue, he shrieked in pain.

She reached to her garter and yanked out her derringer. He aimed his Colt at her. Each stared down the barrel of the other's weapon. Blood dripped down his chin, felt as though she tore his face off.

"You bitch! I don't know what it is that makes me love you! You're just a tramp with cheap perfume! I hate you for what you've done to me!"

"What cheap perfume?" she countered. "It came from Paris, France—the best money can buy! What d'you know about perfume? You're a stuffed shirt with a fast tongue, but I know the truth about you. You're just another flimflam man, and when it comes to bed, you're as bad as they get!"

Her words struck at the core of his masculinity, he lost control. He aimed his gun at her and pulled the trigger. She fired at the same instant. The room reverberated with the sound of gunfire, both bullets missed. Jamie Boggs appeared in the doorway, blood flowing down the side of his face. He lunged in front of Belle, as Madden fired again.

Jamie felt a sharp punch to his solar plexus. Belle fired over his head, her bullet cut a red swath through Madden's hair. Jamie fell to the rug, Madden landed two seconds later.

Belle stared at them, smoking derringer in her hand. Blood foamed from Jamie's mouth, his body shaken by tremors, blood welled out of his chest. He tried to say something, suddenly went still.

Gasping for air, she took a step back. Her servant gave his life for her. A pool of blood lay underneath Bart's head. She believed she killed him. Stunned by the sudden deadliness of the shootout, she reached for the bottle of whiskey and guzzled a quarter of its contents.

10

STONE RODE AT the front of the posse, his sharp eyes scanning the terrain, a far cry from the Great Plains where a man could ride hundreds of miles flat in any direction.

Here were forests, mountains, passes, box canyons, sinks, and ravines to block a man's progress. A waterfall fell down the side of a mammoth eminence, the sun casting a rainbow through the spray. Slipchuck scouted several hundred yards ahead of the main posse. They didn't need a war party of Shoshonis to rip off their hair.

Stone turned in his saddle and looked at his men. Not trained soldiers, many drunk, riding for reward money and plunder, they'd break and run if the fight turned hot. He wondered about turning back, but Kincaid tried to murder him and who knew where their paths would cross again? *Best take care of that son of a bitch now. If the men follow my orders, we can defeat them.*

Stone knew cavalry tactics front to back, learned not in books but on the great battlefields of the Rebellion. Hoofbeats of the posse's horses reminded him of army life. He loved the special cadence of massed cavalry on the move.

When the Hampton Legion rode into battle for the first time, the prettiest girls in Virginia lined the road and threw garlands at the gallant young men. On that unforgettable day, Stone wore a spiffy new uniform, brass and leather gleaming, Confederate cavalry hat jaunty on his head. The officers of the Hampton Legion came from the creme of South Carolina society, Wade Hampton one of richest planters in the South. Bands blared and children danced alongside the horses.

Sometimes a young belle would wink or smile, throw a flower or ribbon, do something special to attract his attention. Secure in the nobility of their cause, the big boys rode to war.

Stone never read official statistics, but estimated only about a third of the old Hampton Legion survived. And the girls from nice families who cheered them on? You ran into them in every saloon.

Stone sank into a dark mood. *What was it all for? Here I am playing war again, when I should be on the train to San Francisco.*

A jagged bolt of lightning rent the sky, followed by a peal of thunder. Stone looked at gathering gray clouds. Nothing like a gunfight in a storm. Large drops of rain splattered his old Confederate cavalry hat. *Maybe this posse's a mistake.*

"A lone rider's comin' up the trail!"

Kincaid opened his eyes. He'd been snoozing on the couch behind his wife's cookstove, while she baked muffins for the supper meal. He raised himself to a sitting position, pulled on his boots, reached for his rifle. She pulled hers down from the rack and jacked the lever. He put on his hat and ran to the front porch.

Rain pelted the carpet of brown and red leaves in the corner of the valley. A herd of nearly fifty mixed cattle grazed in a field nearby. Approaching hoofbeats, Kincaid wondered who it could be. *Nobody rides that hard in weather like this unless it's trouble.*

A mounted figure appeared out of the mist, feet flapping up and down against the stirrups, whipping his horse's rump with his reins. He raced across the courtyard, pulled back the reins, jumped out of the saddle before his horse came to a full stop.

Twimby limped toward Kincaid, the stump of an arrow sticking out of his leg. Kincaid took his arm and helped him into the house. Twimby dropped onto a chair. Dolly handed him a cup of hot coffee. He gulped it down, then turned toward Kincaid and said through boiled vocal chords:

"Somebody ratted on you. John Stone and a posse are on their way here right now. You'd better clear the hell out while you got the chance, and for Chrissakes take me with you. If he finds me here, he'll string me up."

Kincaid stared out the window at blinding sheets of rain. Startled for a moment, his crafty calculating mind resumed command of the situation. They had two choices. Run or fight. "How far back would you say they are?" he asked Twimby.

"Maybe two hours. Three at the most."

Kincaid thought of Davis Pass, a trail wide enough for a single file of riders. Walls on both sides had ledges and ridges to conceal an ambush. That'll be the end of the posse.

A small figure in a black cape rode a big-boned white mare across a field covered with knee-high brown grass. Rain whipped and lashed Belle's face, she could barely see, but dug her spurs into the animal's withers and hung on. "God, I'll be a goddamned *nun* from now on if you get me to him in time!"

Her golden hair a matted yellow mop, soaked to her skin, she prodded her horse onward. Rain, tears, rouge, and mascara ran together and streaked her face like a mask of death.

The figure of the preacher lady appeared before her on the muddy trail. "Whore of Babylon, you betray Kincaid for John Stone today, but who'll you betray John Stone for tomorrow? Your deepest love is on sale to the highest bidder!"

"It's not true!" screamed Belle, alarming the white mare. It pounded its hooves into the ground and increased speed. The preacher lady disintegrated in the middle of the trail as the horse splattered through swaying gray curtains of rain.

Bart Madden opened his eyes with the worst headache of his life. He tried to move and the pain got worse, Jamie Boggs lay on the floor nearby, shirt soaked with blood and gore.

Madden rolled to his feet, raised himself. His head felt as if somebody cracked it with a hatchet. He staggered to the mirror. A red furrow parted his hair. He remembered Belle shooting him at point blank range. Got to get out of here.

He paused to look at the bed where he and Belle spent so many happy hours. A sickening sensation in the pit of his stomach, he staggered to the stairs. On the second floor, whores looked at him curiously. A slow day, all males in the hills searching for gold, nobody wanted to ask about shots on the third floor.

"You seen Belle?" he asked one of them.

"Left 'bout an hour ago."

Madden came to the street. A light rain fell. Men carrying picks, shovels, and other mining implements walked toward him from the railroad station, as the whistle blew and the train headed toward San Francisco. The first contingent to respond to news of the gold strike, hordes would follow after the *Lodestone Gazette* hit the big cities of the East, and Madden knew where they'd put their money. In the vault of the Lodestone Savings Bank. When full, he'd transfer it to a bank in Europe, live happily ever after.

Behind the cage, tellers counted deposits. "A better than usual day, sir," said the head teller. "What happened to your head?"

"Tell Doc White to come to my office."

Madden lay on the sofa beside his desk and closed his eyes. The shootout in Belle's bedroom unhinged his mind. Confused, apprehensive, assailed by dread phantoms, he wondered how to proceed.

Kincaid peered at Davis Pass from the valley on the northern end. The rain nearly stopped, sky dark and boiling, he divided his men into two groups. One would establish positions on the east side of the bluffs. The other group, led by him, would dig in on the west side. When John Stone and his men rode through, shoot them like fish in a barrel.

"Don't anybody fire till I give the signal!" he ordered. "We can't let anybody get away!"

The riders separated and rode toward their respective positions. John Stone had to pass through if he wanted to reach the hideout. They hobbled their horses out of sight in a heavily wooded ravine, climbed into nooks and crannies that afforded a clear field of fire to the narrow trail below.

Kincaid removed a brass spyglass from his saddlebags and focused on rolling foothills to the south of the bluffs. Scanning back and forth, searching for movement signaling the appearance of the posse, he spotted something in the corner of his glass.

A lone rider advanced toward the pass. *We're just in time.* He raised his spyglass an inch and saw the main posse. Come into my parlor, said the spider to the fly.

Slipchuck reined his horse, and she performed a dance, wagging her head from side to side. Named Gertie, she was half-wild, but the old stagecoach driver of the plains preferred a mount with spirit. Perfect spot for a bushwhack, Slipchuck thought, eyeing the pass. *Wouldn't go through if you paid me.*

He studied the terrain on both sides. Might travel days without finding another way north. Could get seriously lost in unfamiliar mountain country. Let Johnny worry about it.

Slipchuck trotted back to the posse. Kincaid frowned from atop his mountain aerie. The old fart suspected something. "Keep yer heads down!" he hollered to his men.

John Stone stood in his stirrups, watching Slipchuck return. He examined the landscape for signs of injuns. "Stay ready, men! Something's up ahead."

Slipchuck approached at a canter. The men crowded around Stone. Slipchuck pulled back his reins, came to a halt before Stone.

"There's a pass up ahead," Slipchuck said, "and I don't like the looks of it. If I was going to bushwhack somebody, that's where I'd set it up."

"Another way to get through?"

"Didn't see one."

Stone found their approximate location on the map. A solid mountain range for days in each direction. "I'll ride forward and take a look for myself."

Slipchuck rested his arm on his saddle horn. "I wouldn't ride out there if'n I was you, Johnny. Them hills give me a bad feeling."

"It's probably the bottle of whiskey you drank this morning."

Slipchuck muttered something unintelligible beneath his breath. Stone wheeled his chestnut roan and headed toward the pass. The afternoon was silent except for the clopping of his horse's hooves. A cool breeze passed over the valley. Stone gauged the height of the cliffs, width of the corridor. Fight a war on terrain like this, you'd have to take it mountain by mountain. Many battalions of engineers required to build bridges over rivers and deep plummeting gorges.

Stone gazed at ridges and ledges where men could conceal themselves. Send the posse on foot into the mountains, make sure they were clear, a time-consuming and disagreeable task. If outlaws were holed up, they'd have the high ground. *Maybe it's time to catch the next train to San Francisco, and to hell with Kincaid. We'll never see each other again in our lives, so what's the point?*

Through his spyglass, Kincaid examined the man riding toward him. He focused the brass tubes for a sharper look. John Stone! He squinted to make sure. Kill the son of the bitch while you've got the chance.

Kincaid lay in a low-ceilinged cave, the front stock of his Sharps rifle resting on a rock. He lined up the sights on John Stone, held his breath. The trigger one sixteenth of an inch from tripping the hammer, John Stone careened out of Kincaid's line of fire. Kincaid raised his head to see what happened.

A lone rider debouched from a stand of trees to the east of Stone. Kincaid tried to fix Stone in his sights again, but Stone's horse galloped toward the new arrival. Kincaid picked up his spyglass and caught the rider in his sights.

Belle McGuinness! Stone's horse slowed as she drew closer. Kincaid pulled the rifle butt into his shoulder and hunkered down for another long shot at the man who took his job.

Hysterical, her face smeared with cosmetics, Belle approached on her white mare. "Go back! He's a-gonna bushwhack you!"

"What're you doing here?" he asked, astonished to see her.

She came abreast of him, her clothes damp from rain, her perfect coiffure awry. "Get away!" She raised her reins to whap Stone's horse on the rump.

He grabbed her hand. "What's wrong with you!"

"Kincaid—he . . ."

She jolted in her saddle, eyes round with surprise. A red spot appeared near her collarbone, the sound of a shot echoed across the valley. A second bullet whizzed past Stone's left ear. Belle leaned toward him, he lifted her out of the saddle and kicked his spurs.

The chestnut roan bounded away. Bullets flew around Stone, but he was a moving target. The posse fired over his head at the outlaws in the mountains. In a burst of speed, the chestnut roan placed Stone and Belle on the main trail.

Belle moaned softly in Stone's ear, her blood stained the front of his shirt. *If she hadn't come along, I'd be dead right now.* A bullet whistled past Stone's hip as the chestnut roan galloped toward the posse.

Kincaid spat in disgust. *Posse knows where we are.* He crawled out of the cave and cupped his hands around his mouth. "Back to the hideout!"

The outlaws emerged from their holes in the ground. They descended the hill, heading toward the ravine where their horses were hobbled. Kincaid was furious with himself. *How could I miss?*

He cursed under his breath. *I don't think things out. What a dumb move. Why didn't I wait?*

The men from the posse lay on their stomachs and fired rifles at the mountains. Stone rode closer, held Belle tightly, her body lifeless and arms hanging loosely down her sides. He reined in the chestnut roan, Slipchuck and McGeachy took Belle and gently laid her on the ground.

Stone dismounted and knelt beside her. Slipchuck poured water onto his bandanna and washed the cosmetics from her face. Her breath came in short gasps, an inferno raged in her lungs, she grimaced at the searing, grueling pain. McGeachy placed his saddlebags underneath her head.

She opened her eyes. "Are you all right . . . Johnny?"

"Sure I am, thanks to you, Belle."

"We'll go to . . . Texas together . . . won't we?"

"I'll work the cattle, you take care of the business."

"You won't . . . leave me, will . . . you?"

"Not me, Belle."

Dying, blood leaking out the corner of her mouth, she touched her hand to his cheek. "You was . . . my love . . ."

Her voice trailed off. She stared lifelessly at the sky. He looked at the mountains on both sides of the pass. They'll pay for this. His mind switched into military mode. *What would I do if I were Kincaid? I'd pull out and go into hiding until everything settled down. Maybe the posse can ride through the pass now and catch the outlaws on the other end.*

"Slipchuck, you stay with Belle! The rest of you saddle up and come with me! We'll get behind them and cut them off!"

He took one last look at Belle, then ran and leapt into his saddle, turned the chestnut roan toward the mountain pass, charged.

The posse followed him, slapping leather. The beautiful courtesan lay at Slipchuck's feet, her face white marble, shirt a puddle of blood, eyes glazing over, growing cold. Yesterday she'd been the toast of the town, tomorrow she'd rot in her grave. Slipchuck recalled the bold boss of the Grand Palace swaggering through the corridors, cheroot in her dainty fingers. Now she was dead meat.

At least she makes a purty corpse. When I die, I'll be so ugly they'll bury me quick as they can. He reached forward and closed her eyes. Now she appeared asleep, except for blood coagulating on her shirt. He unlashed his bedroll, covered her with his blanket. Then he clasped his hands together and bowed his head. "Lord, please take good care of Belle McGuinness. She was a good gal, an' I know you'll like her if you just give her a chance."

Kincaid half ran and half slid down the mountain, slippery and treacherous with newly fallen red and gold leaves. He cursed himself for missing John Stone, even for firing at him in the first place. Should've stuck to the original plan.

His heart pounded wildly in his chest. He ordinarily didn't do much exercise, had to pause beside a pine tree to catch his breath. His men crashed through the tangled underbrush nearby. Kincaid felt a terrible premonition.

He pushed himself forward and moved unsteadily down the hill, knees surprisingly weak, afraid he'd fall. He wanted to throw his rifle away, but might need it later.

Why didn't I wait? We had them where we wanted them. Hadn't been for Belle, would've killed the son of a bitch.

John Stone led the posse across the winding trail, heading for the pass in the mountains, ground trembling beneath their hooves, like cavalry at war. Stone charged the entrance, gun in his right hand, reins in his left, his horse galloped through the narrow twisting corridor. Horses behind him kicked up dust and stones as they galloped around curves. Rock walls rose straight up beside them, echoing the roar. Stone saw open sky straight ahead. The chestnut roan ran out the far side of the passageway, Stone glanced to his right and left, no sign of outlaws. He held his hand in the air. "Take cover!"

Kincaid and his men rode down the narrow winding mountain trail, heading toward the main trail leading back to their camp. Furious with himself, chagrined that his soft life was over, Kincaid vowed to retire when things settled down. *Gittin' too old for this stuff.*

They came to the wide trail near the entrance to the pass. Kincaid held up his hand, his men settled down. They listened, heard nothing. Stone and the posse were probably on their way back to Lodestone for help. By the time Stone got there, he'd find the charred ruins of the hideout.

Leaves fell lazily from trees. A squirrel chattered on his branch. The outlaw band formed a column, three men riding abreast, Kincaid rode in front, leading them back to the hideout.

One of the outlaws said, "You should've waited till they was in the pass, Bill. Why'd you shoot?"

"Thought I could stop 'em if I killed John Stone. You boys want a new boss, I'm ready to step down. It was a dumb mistake."

Kincaid never talked like that before. They'd become soft due to their easy life, all their robberies successful so far. They neared a bend in the trail.

Stone and his posse, concealed by trees and bushes, heard the approach of the outlaw riders. They raised their rifles and sighted in. Stone hid behind a massive boulder. The outlaws came into view, Kincaid in front. Stone ducked his head, his rifle cocked and ready to fire. The score would be settled at last.

The outlaw gang twenty yards away, they didn't notice guns aimed at them. Onward they plodded, on the dodge once more. Kincaid tried to cheer them up. "Always wanted to hit an Army pay wagon," he said. "We'll go up to Fort Logan an' get rich."

Something moved in front of him. John Stone stepped out from behind the boulder. "Raise your hands, or we'll shoot you down!"

The forest bristled with barrels of guns. Surprised outlaws raised their hands and glanced around fearfully. Kincaid jammed spurs into his horse, the animal leapt toward John Stone, who fell back out of the way.

Kincaid sped past, yanking his gun. He turned in his saddle and aimed at Stone's badge. The dirt exploded next to Stone's boot. He ran three steps and leapt into his saddle.

The chestnut roan stretched out long legs, Stone sped down the trail, following Kincaid. He rammed his rifle into its scabbard and pulled a Colt.

Kincaid aimed his gun backward, squeezed off a shot, but his horse bounced him around, the bullet rocketed into the sky. Stone fired a bullet wide of the mark. Kincaid rounded a bend, Stone came after him, gaining steadily.

Kincaid turned for another shot, squeezed the trigger. The gun fired, he couldn't hit Stone, but lead might scare him away. Stone leaned against the chestnut roan's mane. "Go get him, boy. We're almost there."

Stone drew closer. Wind whistled through the creases of his old Confederate cavalry hat and washed his cleanly-shaven cheeks as he drew a careful bead on Kincaid's back. Kincaid fired another unsteady shot, then desperation took over. He aimed at the center of the chestnut roan's chest, pulled the trigger. Before his gun fired, something sharp and hot pierced his left kidney, he gasped in pain, his bullet struck a tree beside the trail. The black stallion continued his frenzied dash toward safety, Kincaid tried to hold on despite violent agony. Blood spread over the back of his shirt and seat of his pants, he dropped his gun and leaned to the side.

Stone pulled back his reins as Kincaid fell out of his saddle. The ex-marshal of Lodestone hit the ground, bounced, and rolled. Stone ran to his side, gun ready to fire. Kincaid lay on his stomach, face in the dirt.

Stone pushed the outlaw onto his back. Kincaid looked up and wheezed. Stone detached his canteen from his saddle, unscrewed the top, gave Kincaid a drink. Water spilled on Kincaid's face, he coughed, grimaced, bared his teeth. "First moment . . . I ever set eyes on you, I knew . . . you was trouble."

"You should've left me alone. I meant you no harm."

"Din't . . . trust you." Kincaid blacked out, then came back, looked at the man who shot him, felt the need to make his last confession. "Bart Madden put up half the money . . . for Randy LaFollette."

Kincaid went into convulsions, blood dribbled down his chin. The ex-marshal of Lodestone died with his boots on.

11

NIGHT IN LODESTONE, stars twinkling in the sky above the mountains. Bart Madden sat in his hotel room, drinking whiskey out of a glass, looking out the window to the street below teeming with an influx of miners, prospectors, investors, thrill-seekers, adventurers, and whores. Deposits in his bank soared to nearly a half-million dollars in the course of the day.

The future appeared promising. Transfer money to other banks, and by the time they knew what happened, he'd be in Geneva, a respected wealthy gentleman, maybe marry a countess and live in a castle on the Rhine.

Regarding Jamie Boggs, Bart's word against Belle's. The circuit judge was a friend of his. Madden, a pillar of the community, had more credibility than the whore.

He wondered what he ever saw in the vulgar blowsy woman. Too pudgy, drank and smoked excessively, teeth yellowing from tobacco, breasts sagging. How dare she spurn him? He'd find another in Europe, where women understood the meaning of elegance.

He looked at himself in the mirror, his clothing rumpled. He wondered whether to return home and get more suits. *I paid for that house and I'll go there whenever I goddamn please.*

The desk clerk nodded as he crossed the lobby. Madden walked along the sidewalk, hands in his pockets, thinking of

John Stone. *Kincaid'll take care of him for me.*

He felt uneasy on the sidewalk with so many drunken armed men. His hand closed around the derringer in his pocket. *If anybody bothers me, shoot first and ask questions later.*

He approached the front door of his home, turned the doorknob, rapped the brass knocker. "Open up!"

"What do you want?" asked his wife on the other side of the door.

"My clothes."

She unlocked the door. *Why'm I living in a hotel when I own this house?* He thought of forcing Patricia and his sister-in-law to move out, but the banking community might not understand. *Maybe my lawyer can argue that she committed adultery with John Stone. The big dope won't be alive to deny it.*

He climbed the stairs to the second floor and continued to the attic, where he found trunks and suitcases left over from the original trip to Lodestone. He carried them downstairs, stuffed his clothes inside. Tomorrow he'd hire Negroes to carry everything to the hotel. He snickered at his cleverness.

Gail walked by his open door, her adorable face visible for a brief moment. *Now that's what I need, somebody young who can learn, instead of a tainted woman who drinks and smokes cigars like a man. No one respects a woman like Belle McGuinness. Did Gail smile just now?*

She always seemed interested in me, even when we first met. Younger women sometimes are fascinated with older men; once he met a banker fifty-eight years old with a wife twenty-two, the power a successful man wields.

He walked down the corridor and knocked lightly on Gail's door. "May I speak with you?" he asked politely. He pushed open the door and entered her bedroom. Clean underclothes lay folded on the bed, she blushed as he ogled them.

"What do you want?"

He held his lapels and planted one foot in front of the other, taking a stance he thought made him appear heroic and appealing to the female mind. "We like each other, and I think it's time we came out and admitted it." To his jaded eyes, she feigned confusion and innocence. "I realize it's difficult for a young inexperienced woman like you to admit something like that, but I understand." He moved closer and held out his arms.

She pressed her back against the wall. "Don't come near me."

He thought she was leading him on. "You're so beautiful," he murmured, bending toward her delightful little earlobe.

"Get away from me!" She slapped his face with such strength his head spun to the side.

"You little bitch!"

She raked her fingernails across his cheek, he caught her with a left hook to the jaw. She crashed against the wall and fell to the floor. The door flew open, Patricia stood there with a loaded double-barreled shotgun. "Touch her and I'll kill you!"

"Not what you think—she was tempting me," he replied. "Had to stop her. You don't know your little sister as well as you think."

"Get out of this house, and don't come back. If you want your clothes, send somebody."

He gauged her eyes, trying to see if she had sufficient courage to pull the trigger, decided she did. "This isn't like you, Patricia."

"Start walking, and don't make me mad. I might kill you by mistake."

She followed him into the corridor. The aunt who raised him spanked him with a board. His schoolmarm cracked him over the head with a ruler. Slimy castrating creatures. At the bottom of the stairs, he turned and faced her. "If only you knew how much I hated you, you whimpering, simpering fat pig. I never loved you, even at the beginning. You were just something I used, until I could find something better. Who could ever love you?"

Her hands trembled, she struggled to prevent herself from killing him. "I can lose weight, but you'll never be anything but a lowdown sneaky skunk."

"You know what I hate most about you? You don't have a brain in your head. I've had many lady friends, you never even suspected." He recited names, her eyelashes fluttered, she appeared faint. Her closest friends!

"You're a liar!"

She became distracted for a moment. He rushed forward, yanked the rifle out of her hand and, hit her in the head with the butt. Her knees gave out, she went crashing to the floor.

"How dare you defy me?" he asked, a strange glitter in his eyes. He placed his fingers around her throat.

Tyrone walked across the backyard, scratching his empty stomach. He hadn't eaten all day, maybe the nice white ladies would feed him again. If not, the baker might give him some stale bread.

A warm glow came over him whenever he thought of yesterday, the plate of food and motherly affection. A poor homeless boy sometimes needed the affection more than the food.

I'll ask 'em if'n they needs any work done. Don't want nothin' fer nothin'. I can wash the dishes if there's a box they can stand me on.

Knee exposed through the hole in his pants, shivering in the cool night air, on his way to the front door, he passed a window. His eyes widened, he opened his mouth and screamed: "Halp!"

Madden glanced up. Letting Patricia's throat go, he grabbed the shotgun and ran to the window. A little boy sped off through the night, waving his arms and hollering at the top of his lungs. Madden knew, in that instant, his life was over. Angrily he bashed the window with the butt of the shotgun, then turned it around, aimed wildly, pulled both triggers.

The shotgun sounded like a cannon on the still October night, reverberating off the walls of buildings. Madden pulled back, blew out the lamp above the fireplace, knelt beside his former wife.

She was dead, thumb impressions around her throat where he'd strangled her. He felt happy, frightened, aware he'd gone too far. But hatred for the namby-pamby bitch overcame his reasoning.

He wondered what to do. *Can I talk my way out of this?* He snapped his finger, the perfect story came to him. No marshal in town, a thief broke into his house and attacked his wife. Madden tried to save her, the attacker ran away, Madden fired the shotgun but missed.

Two witnesses could contradict him: the little boy and Gail. A lawyer would tie the little boy in knots on the witness stand, and Gail, maybe the intruder killed her too?

Madden climbed the stairs, a grim smile on his face. *I can think circles around anybody in this town. Wouldn't be anything here but gophers, it weren't for Bart Madden.*

A crowd of late-night revelers watched the strange procession advance down the main street of town. John Stone rode in front of the posse, with Slipchuck to his left and Kevin McGeachy to his right. Behind them, Belle McGuinness and Bill Kincaid were tied head down over their saddles, Belle's long blond hair trailing in the mud.

The posse came to the stop in front of the marshal's office. They climbed down from their saddles, threw reins over the hitching post. "Take the bodies to Dr. White," Stone said.

Slipchuck and two other posse members led the horses bearing dead toward the doctor's home. Stone entered his office and took a double-barreled shotgun down from the wall. He loaded it, stuffed his pockets with additional cartridges.

"Who you a-gonna shoot?" McGeachy asked.

"Bart Madden."

Stone walked out of the office, shotgun cradled in his arm. A miner lay unconscious in the gutter, the deserted street illuminated by light filtering through saloon windows. Stone stepped over the miner and headed toward the Madden residence. His lips compressed to a thin line, he thought of Belle and Kincaid lying side by side in the coroner's examining room.

Less than twenty-four hours ago he made love to Belle. He hadn't bathed since, her perfume still clung to him. He couldn't quite accept that she put her life on the line for him. No woman, not even Marie, ever made the supreme sacrifice. *She loved me, I used her.*

"Johnny?"

Edgar Faraday teetered in front of a saloon, notebook and paper in hands. "Saw you pass by. Posse back? How's about your exclusive story for the *Lodestone Gazette*?"

"Ask somebody else."

"You're the man who shot Randy LaFollette. My readers want to know about you."

"Write about me, a thousand lunatics'll try to shoot me down."

Faraday made a face of exaggerated mock indignation. "You

wanted to print the truth about other people, but I can't tell the truth about you?"

"Something I got to do."

Stone's spurs jangled every time his boot heels hit the sidewalk. Plinking pianos could be heard through closed windows of saloons. *Wish I sat down with Kincaid and had a talk. Could've settled everything, but he was afraid I'd give him away.*

Stone stepped over another miner lying unconscious on the sidewalk. He heard footsteps across the street. A scrawny little Negro boy dressed in rags ran toward him.

"Marshal . . . Marshal . . ." The boy waved his arms excitedly in the air.

Stone tossed him a coin. "Buy yourself a steak."

"Marshal . . . Marshal . . ."

Stone reached for another coin. "Get some food for your brothers and sisters while you're at it."

"But, Marshal . . . Mr. Madden done kilt his wife!"

Bart Madden lit the lamp in the bedroom. Gail drew herself to her hands and knees on the carpet, a black and blue bruise on her forehead where he'd crowned her previously. She glared at him in half fear and half anger. He pointed the shotgun at her. "Stand up."

She rose unsteadily to her feet, held the bedpost for support. The room spun around. "Where's my sister?"

"A thief broke into the house and killed her."

Gail hoped she hadn't heard what he said. Head pounding, she sat at the edge of the bed. *This isn't really happening.*

"It was the same burglar who knocked you out. Don't you remember?"

"You're the one who did that," she said.

"It might be best if you forgot. Otherwise . . ."

He aimed the gun at her. Hair rose on the nape of her neck. *Say anything he wants. Do whatever he asks. The longer you talk, the longer you live.* "Yes," she said shakily, "I see what you mean." She forced a smile, hoped it looked enticing. "With Patricia gone, you can marry her sister, isn't that so?"

A sigh escaped his lips. "I've been right all along. You cared for me even at the beginning?"

"You have the nicest smile."

"Darling," he said, reaching toward her.

She aimed a careful kick at his most sensitive spot, but he saw it coming in time, wiggled to the side, her toe connected with his thigh. He dived onto her and pinned her hands to the bed. "You little idiot!"

She struggled against him. He felt her young lithe body, wished he had two more hands. *I'll say the burglar killed both of them while I was out cold on the floor.* He let her hands go and pulled his derringer. She shrank from his ugly .32 caliber weapon. He arose from the bed.

"You're a very stupid little girl. We could be happy, if you'd see me as I really am."

She balled her fists and said, "I do see you as you are! You're a madman! You'll never get away with this!"

"Of course I will. You and your sister were murdered by a thief. No one'll suspect Bart Madden, the man who made Lodestone."

She realized he was right. *He'll get away with it. Have to do something.* Again, she forced a smile. If it worked once, might work again. "You're a bad man, Bart Madden, but you sure know how to think."

"You don't know half the story." He pointed to his head. "I made Lodestone out of my brain."

"Patricia never really appreciated you."

"She thought she was a match for me, who built a town where was nothing but trees before."

Her mind raced for something to say. If only someone would knock on the door. "You could do anything you wanted. A man like you could be President of the United States. The woman who ends up with you would be lucky."

"Could've been you."

"I see you in a different light now. You fascinate me. I wouldn't mind living in luxury, and as for Patricia, we weren't as close as you thought."

"Don't lie to me, Gail. Do you really think a silly little goose like you can fool the man who built Lodestone?"

"I'm young and inexperienced. You could teach me things. I'd do anything you said."

"I don't believe you." He raised the gun.

"Give me a chance," she pleaded. "Tell me to do something, and I'll do it."

Something unraveled in his mind. A beautiful young virginal woman offering herself? He aimed the derringer at her. "Take off your clothes."

The Madden residence was dark except one light behind the curtain in an upstairs room; Stone crouched in an alley and took stock of the strategic situation. Armed townspeople surrounded the house. The word spread like wildfire: Bart Madden murdered his wife and held young Gail Petigru prisoner.

Both chambers of Stone's shotgun loaded, he wondered what was happening in that upstairs room. He slipped out the alley and moved toward the house, taking advantage of every shadow and dark spot for concealment.

He jumped the backyard fence, disappeared, his head popped up dimly near the front door. Stone reached for the doorknob, turned gently. It clicked. He pushed the door open and entered the dark vestibule, aiming the shotgun straight ahead.

"Now remove your blouse."

Madden's voice came from the second floor. Stone crept to the stairs. A dark figure lay on the sofa in the living room. Stone climbed the steps, careful not to creak the floorboards. Like a phantom he moved down the hall.

Madden sat in the chair, legs crossed, foot bouncing up and down as he gazed at Gail in her chemise and knee-length underpants with frill on the bottoms. "You're so precious," he said. "Please remove the chemise."

No one except her mother ever saw her bare breasts, but what are bare breasts compared to life itself? Her fingers reached toward the tiny top button.

In the hallway, Stone paused beside the door. He didn't like the silence. A shotgun blast in a small room might hit Gail. He lay the weapon down and pulled both his Colts. Aiming straight ahead, he stepped into the room.

Madden saw him out of the corner of his eye. Before he could move an inch, Stone's right Colt fired. Madden's hand felt as if hit by a hammer, he dropped the derringer.

"Don't move!" ordered Stone.

Madden leapt out of the chair. Stone fired a barrage at the warm cushions Madden left behind. Fabric, wood, and cotton batting exploded into the air. Madden yanked out his penknife, grabbed Gail with the strength of a madman, held the blade to her throat.

"Drop your guns, or I'll kill her!"

Stone let his Colts go.

"The knives in your boots, on the floor too."

Stone pulled the knives, they clanked to the rug. "Don't hurt her. She didn't do anything to you."

"You want the girl alive? Get me a horse."

Gail's eyes looked at Stone pleadingly, her face streaked with tears.

"Just don't hurt her," Stone said.

"Get moving, or she dies."

Stone walked down the corridor, followed by Madden and Gail with a knife at her throat. The derringer in its deerskin pouch nestled against Stone's chest. *Maybe I can get off a fast shot, but it might hit Gail.* They descended the stairs. Townspeople watched avidly as Stone appeared on the front porch.

Madden pushed Gail ahead. Moonlight glinted on the knife against her throat. Stone said, "Mr. Madden needs a horse!"

"Got just the one," Slipchuck replied, leading Gertie forward.

Madden watched Gertie come closer, knew little about horses, one as good as another. Slipchuck held Gertie's reins. Madden pushed Gail to the steps. They moved toward the animal watching them warily with big luminous eyes.

"Give me your gun," Madden said to Slipchuck.

Slipchuck handed him the Colt. Madden pointed it at Gail. "Get on the horse."

"That wasn't our deal," Stone said.

"I leave her here, you'll pick me off before I go two steps."

"Somethin' you ain't thought of," Slipchuck told him. "Two people slows down a horse. You're better off alone. Be gone a-fore you know it."

Madden held the barrel of the gun to Gail's head and looked at the townspeople gathered around, staring in horror at the prominent former citizen turned murderer. Madden's hair mussed, eyes crazed with deep insanity, he had to ride for his life. "Everybody clear the yard!" He pressed the gun barrel against Gail's temple. "I won't hurt the girl if you do as I say!"

The citizens pulled back to alleys and side streets. Stone crouched behind an apple tree, drew the gold-plated derringer Belle had given him. Madden scrutinized his surroundings one last time, then pushed Gail away abruptly and climbed into the saddle, kicking his heels into Gertie.

The semibroken mare didn't like to get kicked. With an angry whinnie, she hunched her back, nearly throwing Madden from the saddle. He clutched in his heels and gripped the pommel with both hands. Gertie twisted in a circle, humping and kicking. Madden somersaulted into the air, Stone leapt to his feet and ran across the yard. The gun in Madden's hand fired wildly, he dropped to his back, sudden impact knocking the wind out of him. He opened his eyes, Stone touched Belle's derringer to his forehead.

"One move and I'll kill you. You're under arrest."

12

THE WHOLE TOWN turned out for Belle's funeral. Children played tag among gravestones, while parents stood solemnly, many men recalling fond intimate moments with the famous courtesan, most of the women glad she no longer could steal their husbands.

The preacher's voice intoned a psalm. Cinders from the stamp mill smokestack floated to the ground. Stone thought of the time he'd spent with Belle. She gave him everything she had.

I'm bad luck for everybody I ever met. I should leave the rest of the world alone. Plagued with doubts about his actions, guilty for sins of omission and commission, he bowed his head. *I wish I took you to Texas, Belle.*

The band played martial music, flags and bunting fluttered in the breeze. Children had been let out of school for the historic occasion. On the platform, Mayor Ralston shook Tobias Moffitt's hand. "We hope your stay in our fair city has been an enjoyable one, despite certain . . . inconveniences."

Moffitt chomped his cigar. "Thank you for your hospitality, your honor. I can guarantee you, we'll never forget Lodestone."

Stone and Slipchuck stood near the entrance to Moffitt's private car, saddlebags slung over their shoulders. No one could board the car before the vice president of the Kansas

162

Pacific. Ahead lay San Francisco, the famous fabled city on the Pacific Ocean, gateway to China, Japan, Russia, and Alaska, wildest, maddest metropolis in the world.

Muggs growled deep in his throat. Stone dropped to one knee before the squashed bulldoglike face. "Wish I could take you with me." Stone patted his head. "You're a damn fine animal." Muggs barked happily.

Gail Petigru drew near, wearing a long green wool coat with matching bonnet. "Thought I'd say good-bye."

"When're you going back to Bangor?"

"Patricia made me her beneficiary. My lawyer says I might end up with the Lodestone Savings Bank."

"Sell everything and get out of here fast as you can," he advised.

"Thought I might like to see San Francisco."

Stone remembered her shivering in her underwear. "Maybe we'll see each other again."

"Know what hotel you'll be staying at?"

"Probably be married by then."

"I guess a girl has to take her chances."

"I think a girl should go back home and marry a decent man."

"What if the girl doesn't want a decent man?"

"She's in deep trouble."

"Maybe she knows something you don't."

He liked her quick mind. "If we ever run into each other again, I'd be happy to see you."

The train whistle blew. "All aboard for Denver, Ogden, and San Francisco!"

Gail reached up and kissed John Stone's cheek, then turned abruptly and ran away. Slipchuck spat a stream of tobacco juice to the ground. "If'n I was you, wouldn't let that little filly get away."

"You haven't seen Marie Scanlon yet."

Moffitt slapped him on the shoulders. "Let's go to San Francisco, Johnny!"

Stone climbed the stairs to the luxuriously appointed railway car, found a seat near a window. Moffitt and his entourage strolled down the aisle. Stone gazed at Lodestone. Wouldn't be the first boom town that disappeared off the face of the earth.

• • •

Muggs sat beside the rails, watching men load boxes into a freight car. His spotted tail wagged from side to side, his tongue hung down, he breathed excitedly. The big metal caterpillar exuded weird sounds, steam, exotic fragrances. Moved faster than the wind, where did it go?

He thought about the man with the nice smell. Not everybody was kind to the ugly brutish-looking creature, children afraid of him, men smelling of firewater booted his rump whenever they felt like it. The meat plentiful and good, the man a good provider, needed a good dog to watch out for him.

Workers finished loading, lit tobacco. One patted Muggs's head and scratched his ear. "How ya doin', boy?" Muggs watched them walk away. Farther down, people said goodbyes, lined up, boarded the train. Muggs licked his chops eagerly as he tensed.

Suddenly he was off, bounding toward the railway car. He leapt into the air, landed inside, disappeared into the shadows.

Bart Madden sat in his cell, listening to the lonesome train whistle in the distance. He puffed the butt of his last cheroot and gazed out the tiny barred window at the clear blue sky, furious with himself for getting caught. *Gave in to temptation, but how could I resist?*

His most malignant thoughts were reserved for John Stone, humiliating to be tricked by an inferior mind. *Maybe I can beat those charges. Or bribe someone. Or escape.*

He scratched a flea crawling through his armpit, plotted strategies and schemes, they haven't hung Bart Madden yet. *I'm the man who made Lodestone. The world hasn't seen the last of me.*

The train roared through a tunnel, Stone dozed in his chair. He thought of Gail, Belle, Marie, his mother, all the other women who dazzled and tantalized him throughout his life. Since an infant, all he ever did was please women, so they'd love him. His ranch in Texas would be incomplete without Marie to warm his bunk on cold winter nights.

It didn't seem so much to hope for. If Marie were in San Francisco, he'd translate the plan to action. In Texas before

Christmas, they'd decorate a tree as in the old days, make their own baby Jesus.

San Francisco in four or five more days, free transportation all the way, thanks to Moffitt. *Get ready for a ghost from your past, Marie. I'm a-comin', and I'll find you if it's the last thing I do. When I put that engagement ring on your finger, it was for life.*

Slipchuck dug his elbow into Stone's ribs. "You mad at me, pard? 'Cause I was a-gonna stay behind in the Grand Palace?"

"Hell no," replied Stone. "I understand how important a whorehouse can be to an old reprobate like you."

"God wants me to go to San Francisco, to watch yer back. You'll need preteckshun, word ever gets around you're the galoot what shot Randy LaFollette."

"Word won't get around, because we'll keep our mouths shut, right?"

"Don't like shootouts any better'n you, Johnny boy. But don't you worry. God protects an honest cowboy."

"Where the hell was He the last few days?"

"You're still alive, ain't you?"

The train blasted out the tunnel and chugged on steadily toward San Francisco. Stone and Slipchuck shielded their eyes from the sudden onslaught of red-hot molten sun sinking into the Rocky Mountains, golden rays constellated across the sky.

A special offer for people who enjoy reading the best Westerns published today.

WESTERNS!

NO OBLIGATION

Mail the coupon below

To start your subscription and receive 2 FREE WESTERNS, fill out the coupon below and mail it today. We'll send your first shipment which includes 2 FREE BOOKS as soon as we receive it.